The
Fugitive Affair

The Fugitive Affair

A NOVEL OF SUSPENSE

Rosemary Gatenby

DODD, MEAD & COMPANY · NEW YORK

Library of Congress Cataloging in Publication Data

Gatenby, Rosemary.
　　The fugitive affair.

　　I. Title.
PZ4.G26Fu　[PS3557.A86]　　813'.5'4　　76–2740
ISBN 0–396–07312–3

FOR
Mary Mix Foley

Part One

1

On the day his uncle called me at our New York offices, I had
not seen Warren Thayer for three years. Not since well before
he'd dropped from sight. I didn't know, even, whether Warren
was dead or alive.

Oliver Thayer gave no clue to what he wanted to talk to me
about, but I think I guessed. If it were business, a commission
for the architectural firm I work for—to design a new building
for the Thayer Foundation or for the Thayer School of Medicine at Downing University, or a new wing for the Thayer
Museum of Fine Art—he wouldn't be taking the project up
with me; he'd have sent one of his underlings to confer with one
of my superiors.

And there was no question of his coming to see me; I went
over to call on him—on that June day in 1975—at his office in
the all-glass building on Park Avenue that housed the bank the
Thayer family had built up. Or vice versa.

It was a long time, I thought as I stepped into an express
elevator and was transported semi-weightlessly to the seventeenth floor, since Warren and I had reached our parting of the
ways—ideologically first, and then in fact and irrevocably,

when he became a fugitive from justice. But he was still my best friend.

You don't replace the favorite companion of thousands of days of your boyhood; you can cut him out of your life, certainly, or he can drop you from his—but he can never be replaced any more than you can live your childhood over a second time.

Someone else was waiting ahead of me in Oliver Thayer's outer office—a thin man with a gray crew cut, sitting with head bent, studying a sheaf of papers from his briefcase. But I was on some preferred list. "Oh, yes, Mr. Norden!" The pretty, stereotyped face of the receptionist lit up as if a switch had been pressed, when I gave her my name. "Mr. Thayer's expecting you. Go right in."

"Lex!" Warren's uncle rose from behind his desk, a great slab of marble like a grave marker. He met me midway of the lush green carpet which stretched, a grassy meadow, to the far walls of floor-to-ceiling glass.

"Good of you to be so prompt. Pleasure to see you!" He shook my hand, grasped me by the arm, and didn't let go till we were seated, half-turned to face each other, on a long sofa with a backdrop of Park Avenue on the other side of the gray glass.

Cordially he asked how I liked my job with Randell Associates; how my parents and my grandmother were; all those little politenesses. So I inquired, of course, about his son Richie. I'd never seen much of Richie even when we were children, since he was younger than Warren and I, and had always gone with his own kind of friends. But anyone who read the society gossip columns could get a pretty clear picture of him.

"Oh, he's fine. Just finished his freshman year at college. He's away in Italy this summer, making a study of Renaissance art. Eventually it'll be up to him to oversee the acquisition side of things at the museum; he's always had a particular interest, you know, in the collection." He hoped, I'm sure, that this was true.

2

Though if Richard Thayer had an interest in any kind of art other than pornography, I'd have been much surprised.

"I don't suppose you see much of Julie," I said, and realized at once that my phrasing was unfortunate. The cloud that had overlain Oliver Thayer's relationship with his daughter was perhaps an embarrassment to him. I'd never before thought of it from his angle—only from hers.

But he smiled. "I see her often—when she's in town, that is. We have lunch or dinner together. But as you know, she travels so much on that job of hers—"

We came then, very promptly, to the reason he'd sent for me. He was unable to contemplate the matter sitting down, and instead paced restlessly back and forth, and I watched him. A rather tall man, about six feet, with no extra flesh on him. A caved-in sort of face, with great indentations on either side of the forehead and in each cheek, as though fifty years ago the doctor, in order to deliver him, had grabbed his head with a pair of ice tongs, and the marks had never gone away. Not too bad-looking a face at that, for it had an impressive ruggedness, and a pair of penetrating dark eyes that held you in their spell.

He stopped pacing and stood in front of me.

"Warren was seen the other day. In Montreal."

My interest leaped at once. "He's okay, then! That's good news."

He gave me a sharp glance which made me wonder whether he thought it was. But then he said, "Yes. When it had been so long, and no one had heard from him . . ."

One postcard, addressed to his mother. He'd sent that about a month afterward. As far as I knew, no word had come from him since.

"The indictment against him still stands, of course." He sat down again. Flexed his hands, looked at them curiously, and then fixed me with those penetrating eyes.

"That's why I want to talk to you, Alex. Frances has been heartbroken over this thing—as you know." Frances Thayer,

3

Warren's mother. "She's afraid she'll never see him again. And of course I—well, Warren's the only son of my only brother. And ever since Stuart's death . . ." He stared out the window at the building across the street, another glass skyscraper almost a duplicate of this one.

"Alex, would you go to Montreal for us? Find Warren?"

"To what purpose?"

"Tell him we'll stand behind him. If he'll give himself up, we'll get the best criminal lawyer in New York for his defense. We'll get him off."

"He'll never come back, Mr. Thayer. You know that."

His eyes narrowed slightly. "I *don't* know that. I do know there's every reason we can get him off—if he'll stand trial. I've already talked to Murray Greenfield, sounded him out—the best man to handle his case. There's no hard evidence that Warren actually slipped a hacksaw blade to that man when he visited him in jail. The assumption that he did is pure guesswork. And the identification of Warren as the one who shot the state trooper from Lissing's getaway car—that can be shaken. Look, criminals get off scot-free in our courts every day; you can bet a Thayer will, too."

I was remembering the last time I'd seen Warren's uncle. It had been during the Christmas holidays, the year I got my architectural degree from Harvard. He had waylaid me, at a glittering party Frances Thayer gave in the big Thayer house on Long Island's North Shore—the house Oliver Thayer had grown up in but which had of course gone to his older brother.

"Alex," he had said, "can't you do something to knock some sense into Warren's head? Boy's not just far left, he's becoming a damned revolutionary." He was so outraged that his hand trembled, and some of his martini slopped over and dripped on the Aubusson rug.

So I asked now, "Are you sure you really want him back, Mr. Thayer? Back, and cleared, and free to continue his journalistic support of these various revolutionary groups?"

4

A sort of spasm crossed his face, so quick I almost didn't see it. "You know," he admitted, "what I've said about all that. You know where I stand—utterly opposed to everything Warren apparently believes. Or *believed;* who knows what he thinks by this time? But the family is what matters, you see. Frances shouldn't be made to suffer like this. And when I think of my brother Stuart . . . If he were alive . . ."

"You're not planning on some kind of deal if he should agree to give himself up? 'Change your politics, and we'll get you off'?"

He looked at me straight. "No. I'll go on hoping he's learned his lesson, after the mess he got himself into; hoping he'll have moderated his views, gotten a better understanding of the values he's thrown away. If not, of course . . ." He turned away to look out once more through the glass wall into Park Avenue. "Well, he's Stuart's boy . . ." The emotion in his voice surprised me a little. I'd always thought Oliver Thayer was a pretty cold fish.

And "Stuart's boy" was hardly that; he was a little closer to thirty than to twenty, his convictions hardened by nearly a decade in the service of the cause he had espoused.

"I still don't think there's a chance he'll come back," I said.

"It's worth the try. To *me* it is, and to Frances."

"Why not put a private detective on it then? A professional outfit would find him much quicker than I would."

"They might run him down—granted. But he'd never talk to their man. Or to me. The person who told me he'd seen Warren in Canada is an old friend of mine; someone Warren knows well. Harold ran into him almost head-on, by chance, spoke to him by name, and Warren immediately dodged away and disappeared in the crowd. He doesn't want anyone finding him; talking to him. You're our only chance. I don't think he'd run from you."

"I couldn't go right now. I'm working on—"

"Don't tell me that with construction in the slump it's in,

5

you're up to your eyeballs in buildings to design?" He smiled, but I thought his manner condescending.

"The recession's hit us—sure. But we're still competing for what jobs there are."

"Well. But you could get away," he said impatiently. "I could square it with Sam—he's your boss, isn't he?"

"Yes, but I'd rather you wouldn't. I have two weeks' vacation scheduled next month—early July. If I go, I could go then." I'd planned, it happened, to spend my vacation working with some others of us for Hugo Praeger, who next year was going to run for President; after the Vietnam years and Watergate, I strongly felt that Praeger was the man to have in the White House.

"You *will* go—won't you?"

I supposed I would. Warren's claim on me went too far back to be denied—and Praeger's actual campaign was still almost a year away.

"I'll let you know in a day or two. All right?"

"It'll have to be. But while you're considering this thing, Alex, remember you'll not be doing it for me, except incidentally. You'll be doing it for Warren. He mustn't just throw his life away. You boys have been like brothers since you learned to walk, and I know you must care a great deal what becomes of him."

"I do. But I have no influence over him. Warren's going to spend his life in his own way. If he should decide to take the chance and come back here for trial, I'm sure it will only be because he can do more operating in the open, for the cause of revolution, than he can from underground."

A small, grim smile tightened Oliver's lips. "I refuse to believe that blood won't tell—in the end. What the Thayer family has built up, what it stands for . . . He's a Thayer—that must mean something to him—"

Something to expiate, yes—the sin of possessing all that wealth, I thought as I said good-by to the head of the Thayer

6

family and made my way out of his suite of offices, where the man who had been there ahead of me still waited, blowing his nose into his handkerchief, following my departure with his small black eyes—resentful, I imagined, that on my account he'd been kept waiting so long.

I should explain exactly what had happened to Warren that resulted in his taking leave of all he should have become heir to.

He quit his first job, after college, which had been as a reporter on *The New York Post,* to work for a radical underground newspaper being produced in the East Village. He moved out of his family's Fifth Avenue apartment and out of the social circles in which he had always had his place, and went downtown to live. I visited him a couple of times in his stark two rooms—one to work in, with his typewriter on an old kitchen table, and his files and a battered bookcase and stacks of books and magazines littering the floor; the other for living and entertaining, with a mattress on box springs, a couple of mats on the floor, and posters of Castro and Che Guevara on the walls. We never found much to say to each other there, and his friends made me feel like a leper.

Roy Lissing was one of his friends—a tall, skinny, smoldering kind of man who always looked at me as if I should give him some sort of excuse for my being alive.

"Let's see—oh, yes, it's the architect student, isn't it." I was still working for my degree then. "Going to build us a brand-new world, I expect—all shiny and nice for the poor folks. With garages, I bet, underneath. For their cars."

And it was Roy Lissing who started all the trouble. He attempted to gain the release of two black activists by kidnapping and threatening to kill the daughter of the judge who had sentenced them. The girl was rescued unharmed, and Lissing was captured.

When he escaped, while still awaiting trial, Roy sawed his

way out of a barred window, and in the course of getting away badly injured a guard. He was picked up in a car which was later stopped by a state trooper. The trooper was shot and killed.

The vehicle's license number had already been called in on the trooper's radio. The car was Warren Thayer's. And a passing motorist later identified a picture of Warren as that of the man he had seen firing the gun when the trooper fell.

The car had been abandoned shortly afterward. Its owner and the escaped Lissing had vanished.

Indictments against both of them still stood.

In one day, my earnest, funny, gentle friend who had for years trod on the surface of a treacherous bog, this meadow with a seeming fair prospect for the disenchanted, the unfortunate, the lower echelons of human discards, the ethnic unemployables, the middle- and upper-class dropouts like himself, had been sucked under.

I went back to my office. And I called an old college classmate who was now a lawyer.

"Well, that's not my field, you know," David told me.

"Yes, I'm well aware. You're in corporation law."

"And still at the bottom of the heap—I only do dog work. And criminal law—well, you might as well ask me about brain surgery, I'd know as much. But I can ask around."

"Would you? I'd just like an opinion on what kind of chance he'd have of getting off. If he came back."

"God, he really blew it, didn't he." David had known Warren more by reputation than in fact, at Harvard. Though they'd both been in Eliot House.

He promised to let me know what he could find out.

And so I called Warren's mother. I wanted to talk to her before making any decision on this proposition to bring Warren home and get him off.

She was out when I phoned, but she called me back and I

ended up with an invitation to dinner.

"I can't promise Julie for you, I never know what her plans are," she said. That wasn't news; no one had ever been able to predict her plans.

Though Julie was Oliver Thayer's daughter, she'd lived more of the time at Warren's house than at her own. She was Warren's double cousin, as a result, long ago, of the Thayer brothers having married the two Hargreave sisters. After the death of her mother, when she was small, Julie had clung like a limpet to her Aunt Frances. And when Oliver Thayer had had the ill luck—or bad judgment—soon after to marry a woman whom both his daughter and his sister-in-law detested, a state of warfare had commenced which now had continued for nearly twenty years.

Julie had adored her father—or so people told me. Actually I'd hardly ever seen them together, because the times I was with Julie were generally at Warren's house. She'd been about six when Oliver Thayer had remarried. My grandmother has always claimed that Julie would eventually have adjusted to her stepmother if it hadn't been for two things. First—Christine Thayer promptly became pregnant and produced a baby of her own; a circumstance which deflected from her recalcitrant stepdaughter what small interest she had in children. Second—Frances Thayer foolishly and selfishly encouraged Julie in her rebellion; she saw herself as very much the heroine of the affair, supporting her sister's child in her struggles with an evil stepmother. I'm sure my grandmother was right about this—Frances was delighted to have a lovely little girl, almost the same as her own, to fuss over; and at the same time to be able to spite a woman she so disliked.

None of which was of particular interest to me as I was growing up—boys aren't much aware, I suppose, of the characters or behavior of their friends' parents except as either impinges on their own activities. The one effect on my life of the internecine feud was the frequent presence at Warren's house

9

of Julie, in almost the role of his sister.

So I wondered, as I headed uptown that evening, whether Julie would be present. There were few things or people she cared much about—but Warren was one of them.

It wouldn't really matter, I thought, whether or not she was there; Julie Thayer was never my type.

Frances and Julie Thayer lived on Fifth Avenue, near the Frick, when they were in New York; in a large apartment overlooking the park. Frances Thayer was the only one I knew who still had a butler—my own family had long ago given up such ostentation. John let me in—pleased to see me, certainly; he'd been an ally of Warren's and mine from years back.

"Good evening, sir." His plump cheeks, as he smiled, were plumper now than ever.

"Nice to see you, John. It's been a while—"

He ushered me into the library, where Warren's mother sat on an antique velvet-upholstered sofa reading a Gothic novel.

"Lex!" The small blonde woman who was like an aunt to me laid down her book and put out both hands as I crossed the room, and I kissed her on the cheek. She pulled me down beside her.

"How are you, Frances?" She'd years ago insisted I stop calling her Mrs. Thayer.

"Fine, dear." She looked frail, her features too sharply chiseled. The shadows around her eyes were real, not makeup. "I'm so glad you've come!" She was, I'm sure. I represented a happier era, a time before her family had shrunk to its present small size, and her world become shadowed by worry over her son.

"Hello, Lex." A girl's low-pitched voice behind me.

I turned; aware, even before our eyes met, of the creeping feeling of inadequacy which Julie Thayer's presence had always given me. She had the most frightening poise—a glacial calm combined with a sort of amused skepticism.

She had come in from the hall and stood in the doorway,

looking not unlike a cover for *Savoir-faire,* the fashion magazine she worked for, her dark hair falling to her shoulders above the floaty green dress she wore. She gave me a small, tight smile that reminded me of her father.

"How are you, Julie?"

"Much the same, I expect, as last time you saw me."

I grinned. "You sound bored to death. Are things that bad?"

"Oh, Julie's having a wonderful time," her aunt insisted. "She's still working for the magazine, and she loves it." Her job, I knew, was to travel for them, covering what the skiers and bathers and party-goers were doing in St. Mortiz, the Seychelles Islands, and Marbella.

"Aunt Fran says you've come about Warren."

"Yes. Your father talked to me today." I turned to Frances. "You know that he wants to persuade Warren to give himself up and stand trial?"

"Yes. The idea was mine to begin with, Lex. I've pleaded with Ollie and begged him, ever since Warren disappeared, to do something. To search for him, bring him back and get these charges dropped or disposed of. I was certain Ollie could do it . . . But you know how he felt for so long about Warren—his work on that paper and all. Not that *any* of us have ever believed he shot a state policeman! I've always known Warren simply *lent* his car to a friend—some friend of his and of Roy Lissing's—to use to get Lissing out of the state; nothing more than that. Then when his car was seen . . . well, he had no *choice* but to flee until he could be cleared."

Yes, she'd been over the same ground many times before. Every time I'd seen her.

"Oliver was bitter against him for so long. He wouldn't listen to me. The Thayer name and all it stands for is so important to him. *You* know how he is, Lex. But even Ollie—well, he's changed his mind at last. Or maybe I wore him down. When Harold Saunders returned from Canada with the news that he'd

11

seen Warren there, Oliver came to tell me and said he was ready to do whatever I wanted." There was a glitter of tears in her eyes.

"And if he stands trial and is convicted?" I wondered whether she had considered the possibility.

"Oh, but he wouldn't be!" In shock and disbelief Frances looked from me to Julie. She had lived so long in a world where money took care of every problem that she couldn't envisage life on the other side of the law, with its shrunken hopes and limited options. "Oliver assures me . . ."

And I knew Uncle Oliver would indeed make no effort to get his nephew back if he thought there was a chance of his ending up with a prison term; better a fugitive black sheep than a member of the Thayer family behind bars.

Dinner was served in the small dining room. The one with the Chinese decor—black lacquer furniture, blue and gold drapes, Chinese ancestor portraits on walls of pale blue silk, lighted cabinets containing a choice collection of porcelain and jade. Frances entertained me with news and gossip of people we both know—mostly friends who'd lived around Locust Valley, on the North Shore, when I'd been growing up—and Julie talked about her adventures cruising in the Indian Ocean on a friend's boat.

I knew she would be good at her job on the magazine. Julie had always been good at things. She'd won prizes for her photography when still only a kid, and had a story published in *Seventeen* before she even wore lipstick. She was competitive—a top horsewoman, and the best tennis player I knew. She could beat me at chess with her eyes closed.

I still wondered why she had eloped, at nineteen; maybe the kind of thing that's expected of beautiful, headstrong heiresses, but it had seemed out of character for Julie. The marriage had been short-lived; the family had had it annulled, and she'd taken back the name of Thayer.

Warren said at the time that she'd done it out of spite.

We talked of Warren. The old Warren, in the days before he'd become an activist. The Warren with whom I'd traded stamps, collected birds' nests, built a tree fort, swum in the Sound, played tennis. He hadn't liked anyone in authority even then. I'd joined him in countless plots against our teachers, during school days—harmless pranks, mostly, but it was he who initiated them, and you'd have thought, from his dedication, that he was trying at least to win a global war.

We had coffee in the library.

"I'll call you before I leave for Montreal," I promised Frances. Because I'd known, from the moment Oliver Thayer had broached the subject, that I would go.

"Oh, yes, Lex! I'll want to know when you're going. You can take a letter from me, and—" She broke off, the animation fading from her face.

Bitterly, in a tone not at all like Frances Thayer's, she went on. "I was about to say I'd send him a box of homemade cookies." The bitterness was not meant for Warren; it was directed at herself, perhaps, or at the patterns of our lives. She might as well have said, what have mothers ever been able to do for sons . . . Boys had their own pursuits; they grew up and went their ways . . .

From the look in her blue eyes, under the carefully penciled eyebrows, I realized that she did, after all, understand the extent to which her son no longer lived in the world he once had.

"I should tell you—" Frances glanced over at Julie, and then at me, a little hesitantly. "We were in touch with him once, Lex."

"Besides the postcard, you mean?"

"Yes. Someone delivered the envelope by hand—at the magazine, addressed to Julie. So there was no postmark. Warren enclosed a letter for me, to tell me he was all right. And he wanted Julie to sell his coin collection for him. He needed the money."

"When was this?"

"Last summer. He'd gotten along till then, I guess—he sold some of his stock not long before he disappeared, you know, and we've never found out what he did with the money, so I suppose he had some of it with him."

"Aunt Fran wouldn't let me sell the collection, though—"

With a twisted little smile, Frances shook her head and looked down at her diamond rings. She adjusted them on her fingers. "No, of course not. I had all that money Oliver gave me for the big house—it was just sitting there in a savings account—"

"How did you get the money to him?"

"Addressed to some fictitious name in care of general delivery in Detroit. He said not to have anyone try to follow the person who picked it up, because it would go through several hands. I didn't try, naturally—I didn't want anyone to be able to inform the F.B.I. of where he was. And I told *no* one I'd heard from my son. Particularly not Oliver—he'd have been livid."

Julie took me to the door when I left. "How much did she send him?" I asked. "A fortune?"

"No—she was afraid it might go astray, passing through so many hands. But enough to keep him for quite a while. She told him to let her know when he needed more—hoping he'd get in touch again. But we haven't heard since, except for a postcard from Detroit, not even signed, saying thanks."

"Well, at least we know where he is. Probably. Your father could have sent *you* on this trip—why didn't he? You travel all the time anyway."

Her long-lashed green eyes looked up at me. "I could never convince my dear stubborn cousin of anything. You know that. He'd be surprised, I imagine, to hear that I can even tie my shoes now."

"I'm afraid I'm not much better as an emissary. He and I haven't agreed on anything in years, except maybe which brand of beer we prefer. But I'll give it a try. Be good to see old

Badger, anyway." Badger had long been his nickname, dating from a time we had both taken Indian names and lived part of a summer in a canvas tepee we put up in the woods near his house.

"If there's anything I can do to help . . . Anything. Let me know."

"Sure, Julie."

I wondered—again—why we had never hit it off.

She unlocked the three locks on the door and let me out.

2

Three and a half weeks later I arrived in Montreal.

My lawyer friend David had reported to me, not too pessimistically, on Warren's chances of getting off. We met for dinner at the New York Harvard Club, and over a couple of drinks in the bar he filled me in on what he'd been able to learn.

"A lot depends on what Warren claims really happened. Could be he *did* only lend his car. Maybe he can prove he was someplace else entirely when Lissing broke out. You think?" David, who's at least six inches shorter than I am, leaned his elbow on the polished mahogany bar, his pale face resting against his hand, his light hair lying lankly on his head. He still looked like an undergraduate.

"I doubt if he can prove anything like that. Though I won't know till I talk to him."

"As to who fired the gun that killed the state policeman— well, it *does* seem more than likely, doesn't it, that Lissing would have been the one? The witness said the man in the passenger seat fired, across the driver, at the trooper—as he approached the car after he'd stopped them. It was Warren's car, so it seems logical that he'd have been driving."

"Yet Luzkowski, the witness, identified Warren's picture as

16

that of the man who had fired."

David shrugged. "How could he see that well? It was dark —a very dark night. Could have been anybody in the passenger seat. The defense, I gather, would be that Lu—Luzkowski never saw the face of the man at all, that night—that he picked Warren's picture because he recognized it as that of Warren Thayer, *after* the news had already been broadcast on the radio that Warren's car had been the one Lissing got away in. After all, the Thayer family's been photographed for the newspapers —not as often as the Kennedy clan, but still—"

The next day I'd called Oliver Thayer and told him I'd go.

"Good. I've counted on it ever since we talked." The voice cordial, pleased. "There's no way I can properly thank you, I'm afraid; for the whole family. Only thing I can think of to help out is handle your reservations—my secretary can do all that for you. When are you leaving? And you'll fly up, I expect?"

"Thanks, I can manage, myself. And I'll be driving up—it's not all that far."

"Yes, I see. You're leaving when, did you say?"

Two days later I received a letter from the manager of the Regency Hotel in Montreal with the information that a suite was reserved for me, everything laid on, and the red carpet ready, courtesy of Mr. Oliver Thayer.

Nothing I could do about it, and I knew he would pick up the hotel bill, which I didn't enjoy his doing—it made me feel uncomfortable, as if he had bought my services. Maybe he wanted me to feel that way. I don't know. But it was silly for him to pay—my family's not as rich as his, but we're certainly among the more well-heeled in the New York area. And I was going to Montreal to suit myself, not him.

Julie came by my apartment on a Sunday afternoon—just dropped in, she said, hoping I'd be there. She had a letter her aunt wanted delivered to Warren.

"And this is for him, too," she said. "From me."

She took the box to the window overlooking the East River,

17

to the light, to open it and show me. A miracle of a watch. One of the see-through kind with all the works visible: little parts whirring, oscillating; wheels going around. It was a calendar watch; everything on it but the tides.

"If he had a good one, he's probably lost it by now," she said.

"Or stepped on it," I agreed. Warren was the kind of person for whom mechanical things never worked, and who tended to mislay everything but his beliefs.

I asked her to have dinner with me—we could go out somewhere.

"Thanks, but I can't. I'm meeting someone." She smiled in that cool way of hers, as if she found my suggestion amusing, and the reaction put me off her more than ever. Try as I would, I thought as I closed the door after her, the two of us seemed destined to remain poles apart.

Nor was I, of course, close to Warren any more either.

Yet here I was, on a muggy July afternoon, ready to comb Montreal for him.

I'd not driven up till Sunday because I had spent Friday night and Saturday on Long Island with my parents, as I'd promised to do before they took off on the trip they'd been planning to the Far East. It had been a pleasant time.

Montreal had changed. I hadn't been here since I was nine or ten, and wouldn't have known it was the same place, with its overlay of superhighways and interchanges. The tall new buildings, too, corroborated the statistics on the present booming prosperity of the slow, old French-English town I remembered from my childhood visit here with my mother and father.

As I picked my way through the labyrinth of streets in search of the Regency Hotel, I wondered . . . Did I want to stay there? The V.I.P. treatment I would get under the aegis of Oliver Thayer was all wrong for my mission. If I were to find my fugitive friend, it would be better to arrive as anonymously as

18

possible and remain inconspicuous.

So I drove right by the Regency and headed for The Queen Elizabeth, which I knew by reputation to be a large commercial hotel.

It was the height of the summer tourist season, and some kind of convention was booked into the hotel, but they managed to find a room for me. I settled in, on one of the upper floors with a fine view out over the city, and unpacked. Then I phoned the Regency and canceled my reservation there. I'd better inform Oliver Thayer of where I was staying, but there was no rush—I'd have nothing to report for a while.

So what should I do now?

First I went for a walk.

I didn't expect to run head-on into Warren, as Oliver Thayer's friend had—though stranger things have happened. I was simply looking around at the city. While I was out I bought copies of *The Montreal Star* and *The Gazette*—a bunch of old ones from the week before, which the newsstand still had. I wanted a good sampling of the classified sections.

Back in my room, I checked. *The Gazette* didn't carry much under the heading of Personals . . . *The Star* was the one.

BEAUTIFUL Male seeks beautiful young liberal female . . .

REFINED European gentleman, 39, would like to meet bilingual attractive lady 28/35 years old. Must be sincere . . .

ANYONE KNOWING the whereabouts of Mr. Anthony C. Parmenter, ex-seaman (an old friend) . . .

I couldn't place an ad till tomorrow, I saw: Monday to Friday, 9 A.M. to 4:30 P.M. But I wrote one out, on a piece of hotel stationery:

And who knew whether he read the classifieds?

Now I would have to wait for it to be run; wait again for an answer. Which might never come.

Meanwhile I might as well enjoy Montreal . . . I phoned a likely looking restaurant I'd passed while reconnoitering, and made a dinner reservation. Showered, then walked over through the still hot evening. I might have been in Paris; of the passers-by, only the tourists spoke English.

The snails, the onion soup, the tournedos and the napoleon served by Les Deux Frères were all excellent. But it was true, as I'd always heard—vacationing alone in a large city is inevitably lonely.

In the morning I phoned and placed my ad. And then had the whole day and another evening to while away.

"It will appear in tomorrow's paper," the girl had promised in her heavily accented English. I hoped so.

I headed for the old part of the city—Vieux Montréal. Found myself in the Place d'Armes and went into l'Eglise Notre-Dame. It was like nothing I'd ever seen, with its glowing blue interior, and the unique wood carvings—thousands of delicate arches painted gold with red and green and blue, the rich effect reminding me of the Alhambra. (A heretic judgment, no doubt.)

Leaving the church, I passed the home of Les Messieurs de St. Sulpice; across the street its seventeenth-century walls were reflected, I saw, in the glass and mirror façade of one of the new skyscrapers. Old and modern, vis-a-vis.

I wandered through old streets and squares, noting the architectural features of the buildings; stopping occasionally to read a plaque. But I'm not really much of a sightseer. Though my mind automatically classified as to style every structure I passed, my thoughts were on Warren.

The years at Harvard were running through my head. It was at that period of our lives that we'd begun drifting apart. We'd made different friends. While I spent my spare time sculling on the Charles or building up a relationship with one or another of the Radcliffe girls I met, Warren employed his in earnest discussion with groups of glum, heavy people who clustered together behind closed doors or in little knots in the Yard. I joined him and his friends in some antiwar rallies—we were all bitterly against the Vietnam involvement. But Warren went gung-ho into the S.D.S. movement, which didn't interest me at all. When I occasionally ran into him alone, we got on as well as always, but he never seemed to have much time to talk to me.

So we saw less and less of each other, at college. When we were both at home on Long Island things were the same as they always had been.

Luckily neither of us was called upon to go to Vietnam. Warren had asthma. And after my time in college and graduate school, my number never came up.

I had lunch at a café on Place Jacques Cartier—very *Rive Gauche,* very good. Somehow I spent the afternoon—included in it, a trip via the new, ultra-modern subway system—which had stained-glass windows in the stations.

Dinner at an Argentine restaurant, for a change; and finally the evening disappeared.

As I turned off my bedside light at eleven, I thought of Oliver Thayer—possibly fuming, by now, that he couldn't get hold of me. Tomorrow I'd let him know where I was.

Tuesday my ad was in the afternoon *Star.* On my way down from Mont-Royal Park, where I'd been wandering around high

21

above the city, I picked up a copy at a newsstand and hurried back to the Queen Elizabeth—in case a message should come, or my phone ring.

For the first time it seemed possible that Warren and I might actually meet. I wondered, even, as I neared my hotel, when he might last have walked along this street—and found it easy to envision running into him around almost any corner.

. . . If he lived here at all.

. . . He could have been passing through, when he'd been seen before. Or he could have moved on, after the encounter with his uncle's friend . . .

No message, of course, at the hotel. It was much too soon.

Thinking of Warren's uncle waiting in New York for some word, I tore out the ad and mailed it to him, with a brief note:

> *As you can see, I decided not to stay at the Regency —though thanks. I was afraid the V.I.P. treatment which would result from your having made the reservation would attract too much attention.*
>
> *I'll let you know if anything develops.*

I thought of Julie and Frances waiting, also. No need to communicate with them until I had some news. Oliver would relay to them, anyway, whatever he heard from me.

And so I settled down, with a stack of paperbacks, to wait.

The note came the next morning.

The envelope wasn't stamped; must have been delivered by hand.

I slit it open so hastily that the paper it contained was ripped almost in half.

> *Wednesday*
> *Alex—Why are you here? You shouldn't have come. Don't you know this is dangerous for me?*

If you must *see me, wait this afternoon at 3:00*
o'clock in front of the Château de Ramezay. Be sure
you're not followed.

Warren

I could hardly believe it. I'd really supposed I'd sit around
for days and then never hear from him!

If the letter *was* from Warren? . . . Had to be, didn't it? My
ad had been addressed to "Badger," and who but old Badger
himself would know that the recipient of my message was supposed to be Warren Thayer . . .

At a quarter of three I walked through a gate in the fence
enclosing the area in front of the Château de Ramezay—now
a museum—in the old part of the city.

After half of a chase sequence—my half, for I was sure no
one was following me—I felt less like Sean Connery than like
an absolute nut. I had strolled into a department store (Simpsons), hurried down its aisles, ducked out a side door and
quickly caught a taxi from whose rear window I watched in
vain for pursuers. I had then doubled back by subway, taken
another taxi, and finished up on foot, looking carefully behind
me.

Now I walked up and down in front of the chateau—a one-
and-a-half-story stone building with a round, conical-roofed
tower at one end. Trying to look like a tourist, I studied the long
façade with its tall windows all along the first floor, and the
dormers and chimneys sticking up through the roof.

I read the plaques affixed to the stone wall, giving the history
of the building since its construction in 1705. Inspected the
cannon and the two mortars displayed out in front. Tried to
keep out of the way of the knots and clusters of tourists going
in and coming out of the museum.

Three o'clock came and passed.

I paced, or stood in the shade of a tree at one corner of the building. Stared across the street at the Hôtel de Ville—at its formal flower beds, gold door, copper roof turned green. Its clock was five minutes fast.

Three-fifteen. Three-twenty-five. Three-thirty. Did I have the time right? I took out the note again and checked. Yes—three o'clock at the Château de Ramezay. I studied the handwriting; was I sure it was his? I hadn't actually seen Warren's writing since we'd been in classes together at Exeter, I suppose, but the look of this was near enough to what I could recall of his—an uneven downhill scrawl with letters poorly formed.

Maybe he'd changed his mind about coming. Or—it occurred to me, at least—I *had* been followed. And he'd been picked up as he approached our meeting place?

I decided to go into the museum to wait.

It was a historical museum, lots of interesting exhibits, no doubt, but I didn't examine any of them; I hovered near the front windows, watching through them for sight of a long-familiar figure.

At closing time they shooed me out.

Depressed by the vigil which had come to nothing, baffled as to what had gone wrong, I walked slowly away, glancing about as I went, thinking it possible that Warren might step out of a doorway or come from behind and fall into step with me.

I turned down one of the side streets, toward the waterfront.

But it wasn't Warren; it was a girl who came up beside me as I lingered in front of a shopwindow.

"Don't turn your head. Pay no attention to me. I must speak to you."

"Go ahead." I spoke to her reflection in the glass.

"Do you know you're being followed?"

A sudden involuntary tightening of the nerves. Warren was trailing me, then? Waiting to make contact?

"What does he look like?"

"Go into the shop and I'll come in after you."

24

I went in. It was a gallery, rather than a shop. Paintings and sculpture and some ceramic things. The girl joined me in front of a gloomy canvas titled "View of St. Paul Street."

A heavy-faced woman sat in the rear, doing some kind of needlework, but she paid no attention to us.

"May we just browse?" my companion asked in a clear, carrying voice with a bit of Midwestern twang in it.

She studied me with a pair of heavily made-up eyes under dark, straight brows. "You did know, then? That he's following you?"

"I didn't. It's kind of you to tell me. What does he look like?" Unconsciously I noted the details of her appearance, without being interested, really, in anything about her—my attention being on the possible contact with Warren. She was a smallish girl, about five-two; wearing a blue skirt with knitted top, over it a long-sleeved shirt worn like a jacket. The bright Paisley scarf covering her hair was tied at one side; from under it swung a large pair of ugly blue plastic earrings.

"A big man," she said. "Massive." And I had the disoriented feeling of suddenly finding myself in the wrong script, with the wrong characters and someone else's story. Massive? Warren was five-feet-ten and slender . . .

"You're sure he's trailing *me*?"

"Oh, yes. He was waiting for you. Waiting and waiting, and when you left the museum back there, he followed you." She had strange, round eyes, I noticed—almost protuberant.

"Can you tell me any more about him?"

She picked up the carved wooden figure of a wolf; turned it over and examined the price mark on the bottom. "He's well over six feet—maybe six-four. Not fat, but strong-looking; muscular? Like a football player. Dark hair. Face could be anybody's; just a face."

I stepped to the window and peered out from between a couple of paintings on easels. A few people in the narrow street,

25

but no one answering the description she'd given me.

"I don't think you'll see him. He's being careful that you don't."

I turned and faced her. "Thanks very much for telling me. Why did you?"

Her lips curved upwards a little at the corners. "I don't like to see *any*one being stalked or hunted—neither an animal nor a man. At least I could warn you."

"I appreciate it. If—" but she had already turned away.

"Oh, that's all right." Without another glance at me she went out.

I watched covertly for my shadower, all the way back to the hotel. But with so many people passing along the sidewalks, going in and out of buildings, cutting across the streets, it was impossible to pick out anyone who might be keeping an eye on me.

My mission here seemed hopeless now. Warren had not shown up at the place and time he had specified because he, too, had seen the man following me and had stayed clear. Canadian police? Alerted by the F.B.I.? They could even have opened Warren's note this morning, before it was handed over to me . . .

But how could the authorities have gotten wind of my visit here, and its purpose . . . A dozen ways, probably. The Thayer family was always news, and any word about Warren—after the indictment and all the publicity of two and a half years before—would be a big story around New York. One of the Thayers had only to have mentioned my trip to some friend and my confidential project was common gossip.

I went up to my room and waited, in case Warren should try again to get in touch. Ordered dinner from room service and ate it by the window, where I could look out at the nighttime pattern of the city's lights.

The final estranged period between Warren and me seemed by now to have lost reality. As I thought of him the picture of the somber, bearded character who had lived in the East Village had been crowded out by recollection of someone younger—the gamin face I had known all my life, with greenish-hazel eyes sparkling in devilment as the mind behind them planned, always planned something new and ingenious that we should do.

The phone did not ring that night. Nor did any message come.

So sure was I that my plans were sabotaged beyond repair that I could hardly believe it when late the next morning, on inquiring at the desk for mail, I was handed a letter from Warren.

No doubt in my mind, the moment I saw the downhill messy scrawl, that it *was* from him. With a stamp this time—it had come by post. And I knew as I examined it that yesterday's letter had not been his. (From whom, then?)

In case anyone was watching me this morning, I shrugged, as though in indifference to the letter I had just been handed, and shoved the envelope into my pants pocket. I wandered to the newsstand, which was in a tobacco shop off the lobby. There I scanned the racks of magazines, and bought a copy of *Sports Illustrated,* plus a morning paper. As I stepped into an elevator, I gave my best interested scrutiny to the headlines in the paper, at the same time leaning my right hip firmly against the wall of the elevator—precluding any possible attempt to pick my pocket of the unread letter.

How easy it is to fall into paranoia . . . Begin to believe it possible, merely, that someone could have you under surveillance, and waiting figures, watching eyes, plucking hands (perhaps) are everywhere. I managed in one sidewise glance, as I got out at my floor, to fix in my mind the faces of the only other occupants of the car: a girl—young, brown-haired, but not the one who had talked to me yesterday in the gallery; two plump middle-aged women, obviously tourists; a small, thin man with pointed features and carefully combed black hair, who had been

27

standing directly behind me. The doors slid shut; none of them got off.

Not till I reached my room did I take out Warren's letter. There were two envelopes, one within another. The inner one was sealed with red wax, on which was the impression of the head of a Roman gladiator—the design on the cat's-eye ring he'd had since boyhood. I broke the seal and extracted the page of stationery.

Wednesday

Dear Lex,

 Do all exiles read the personals in case someday, just possibly, there could be a message for them? A form of masochism, perhaps, poring over all those pleas from other people to other *people, all strangers I will never know. Some laughs, of course, in those items. I suppose that's why I read them. Few enough laughs around.*

 It must be you, though, who put the ad in. Not someone laying a trap. I wonder, of course, what the "urgent word from home" is. Not bad news, I hope. I can't call you at the hotel—your phone might be tapped. Don't discount the possibility! They badly want Roy and me, you know. Very badly. Even here in Canada, we've had to move on a couple of times.

 At 2:00 on Thursday, go to the phone booth next to St. James the Apostle Church. It's on Ste. Catherine Street near MacKay. I'll call you there. If we miss, try again at 3:00.

No signature. None needed.

But who had written the other letter? And why?

I'd put yesterday's message on the bedside table, by the phone, when I'd gotten back from my fruitless wait. I picked it up now and compared it with Warren's letter. Different paper, to begin with. The writing *suggested* Warren's hand. But it wasn't his. The salutation should have told me, I realized: *Alex*. Warren had never in his life called me Alex.

Who, then? Roy Lissing? They were still together, or in touch at least, to judge from Warren's letter. But Roy Lissing did not match the description of the man who had waited and waited, and followed me. Roy was tall but skinny—not massive. And the girl? It wasn't likely, was it, that a total stranger would come up to me in the street to warn me.

I stuck the earlier note into my pocket. I'd ask Warren about it when we talked on the phone . . . Thursday. That was today.

Poor homesick Warren. It was not like him to admit even obliquely to any trace of sentiment, and yet in his note to me—

At ten minutes of two I arrived at the phone booth.

Two o'clock came and went. Four after. Five after.

He probably wanted to be sure I'd gotten there.

"Vous ne vous servez même pas du téléphone!" a voice said accusingly. A thin, nervous-looking man of about forty-five, wearing glasses, stood right beside the booth.

"J'attends un appel," I explained.

He switched to English—my accent having no doubt identified me as from south of the border. "And I've got to use this phone!"

I didn't want him hanging around, and possibly listening, when my call did come. It was one of those new-style booths —a round of glass with no door.

I stepped out. "All yours."

He made three calls, while I stood around on one foot and then the other, peering at my watch every fifteen seconds or so, while the traffic whipped by on the other side of the curb.

At last the man left, and I stepped into the booth; slouched against the phone in a listening pose, with the left hand pressing the receiver to my ear, right index finger holding the receiver cradle down. Footsteps went to and fro behind me, but no one

29

else came along wanting to use the phone.

The damn thing rang, and nearly sent me through the glass.

"Yes?" I said.

"Who's this?" Warren; making sure.

"You damn-well know it's me. I got your note sealed with the cat's-eye ring your mother gave you for your twelfth birthday. Want any other identification?"

"You sound mad." No trace of the wistfulness of his letter; he seemed to be amused.

"Some terribly eager salesman wrested the phone away from me and I had to wait while he made all his calls."

"Oh. Listen—I want to see you, too, you know. But can you tell whether you're being followed?"

"Funny you should ask . . . I supposedly got a communication from you yesterday—"

"Yes—go on—" I couldn't be sure whether he was surprised or not.

"A note which came to the hotel, no stamp, so it must have been delivered by hand." I read it to him.

"So you went to the Château de Ramezay—" No comment on the fake letter.

"Yes. And waited till it closed." I told him then about the girl and her story of the man who'd hung around and then tailed me.

"What was this girl like?"

I described her to the best of my recollection.

"What color hair?"

"Dark, I guess. Her eyebrows were very dark. Black. But now that I think of it, I'm not *sure* about her hair—she had it covered with a scarf."

"Humm. Yeh. And did you *see* anyone following you?"

"No. Doesn't prove he wasn't, though."

"No. But let's not worry about that just now. What's this message from home, Lex? My mother all right?"

"She's okay. As okay as possible, that is, considering how upset she is over you. Everyone's all right, Warren—there's no bad news. But your family want you to come home."

A desolate chuckle at his end. "Sure. Great. Why not?"

"Your uncle's got it all set up. He's positive he can get you off. Best criminal lawyer in New York to defend you—"

"No way am I going back!"

"That's what I thought, but let's talk about it."

"Out of the question."

"Going back is? Or meeting to discuss it?"

"Going back's out of the question. And meeting you doesn't seem a very safe idea—do you think? Strange girls wandering up to warn you you're being followed—and you probably are. The pigs would give a lot to get hold of me, finally."

"What about this forged letter? From your pal Roy, maybe?"

"No. Not from Roy. The letter's nothing to worry about. But this character tailing you—I need to check that out."

"I've got to see you, though, Warren. We can manage it somehow—I can shake anyone that's following me. I had practice yesterday, after all—into Simpsons by the front door and out the side five seconds later; jump in a taxi—"

"Who knows you're here, Lex?"

"Your mother, Julie, your uncle. David Kane knew I was coming, but not *when*. Your uncle talked to Murray Greenfield —the lawyer—about the situation you're in—"

"But word can leak out, can't it . . ."

"I have a letter for you from your mother. And a present from Julie."

"I'll tell you where to leave them. Someone will get them to me."

"Warren—listen. I'll be very careful. Tell me where we can meet and I'll take all kinds of precautions to be sure—"

"I'll think about it. Let's see . . . Wait in the phone booth on the corner of Sherbrooke Street and Amherst tomorrow morn-

31

ing. I'll call at eight."

Before I could say anything more, he hung up.

An afternoon and an evening to kill.

I called Oliver Thayer when I got back to the Queen Elizabeth; by now I owed him a report.

He listened. "So glad you've contacted him, Alex—and sooner than I'd expected," he said when I'd finished my account. I asked him who he thought might know of my trip and its purpose.

"I've told no one, Alex, that you were going up there to look for him. I talked to Greenfield, as I mentioned, about the prospects of getting him off, but I said nothing of how I expected to get in touch. I really don't see how the authorities here could have—"

"What about Frances or Julie? They might without thinking—"

"I'll find out. You were right, clearly, about making your arrival up there as unostentatious as possible."

"For all the good that did."

"I only hope he'll decide to see you tomorrow. If you can be sure it's safe. It'll be so much better for his case if he can give himself up. We don't want him being captured before he has the chance. Or shot at, either—my God, I wouldn't want that on my conscience!"

"Yes, I know. Warren won't take any risks, I can promise you. He's been at this hiding game long enough to know how to look out for himself."

"Well, yes."

"So I'll phone you if I can talk him around—or maybe *he* will. Probably tomorrow."

Ten minutes after I had hung up, my phone rang. It was Oliver Thayer again.

"I've just checked with Frances. She tells me she and Julie had agreed not to mention to anyone whatsoever that you intended to go and look for Warren."

"I see."

"Not even John knows. The butler. They've been careful not to speak of it in his hearing—or any other of the help."

"Yes, I know John. Well, thanks, Mr. Thayer."

That left the leak—if there had been one—with me. I had discussed the situation with David Kane. And he, at my instigation, had made inquiries of some other lawyers concerning Warren's situation. Who knew what connections the people in David's firm might have? And the police had only to ask my employers whether they knew of any plans I had for leaving New York—

Oh, hell.

I packed my bag, checked out of the Queen Elizabeth, retrieved my car from the garage, and drove out of the city. Toward Quebec.

3

At a few minutes to eight the next morning I was standing across Sherbrooke Street from the phone booth at which Warren was to call me.

My sense of relief was enormous. *No one* could be tailing me now. Impossible. I'd driven and driven, last night, ending up on narrow country roads with not another pair of headlights either in front or behind. Had turned off my own lights, at last, and pulled into a farm lane, where I'd waited and waited, and no other car had gone by. Repeated this maneuver a second time, before I'd driven back into Montreal, entering on a different highway from the one by which I'd left. Had registered for the night at a hotel that couldn't possibly be listed in the tourist guides—a quite seedy place in the old town. I'd noticed it the day I'd gone to the Château de Ramezay. Hôtel Genève. I was sure no one would have thought to look for me there.

I crossed the street. There were two phone booths, actually. No one was using either; so whichever one rang—

I wondered whether he lived near here. It was a residential neighborhood—two- and three-story stone or brick houses made into flats. Rather scruffy. On the other side of Sherbrooke Street was a little park.

34

He called promptly at eight.

"Look," I said. "If anyone was following me yesterday or the day before, they're not today." I explained.

"Wonderful. No one was following you."

"Oh, Christ! Why didn't you say so yesterday?"

"I wasn't sure."

"So where can we meet?"

"LaFontaine Park. You're right there. Cross Sherbrooke Street, then Cherrier, and continue along the side of the park to Avenue Duluth. Duluth dead ends at LaFontaine Street. Walk into the park, to your right. It's a paved walk. At the drinking fountain it branches. Go to your left and take the first unoccupied bench."

Four minutes later I was sitting on a brown bench overlooking a pond at the bottom of a steep slope. A flight of metal steps went down to the water. The paved path curved away, to my right and my left, and there was good visibility in every direction. Not many people around—it was early yet. Near me there was only a gray squirrel—hopping and then pattering quickly for a few steps over the grass; stopping to sit on his haunches and eye me, sizing me up, probably, as a potential purveyor of breakfast.

And someone else was watching me. I felt it.

The squirrel abruptly abandoned me, departing in long leaps.

Warren came from behind the bench and sat down.

"Lex! How are you?" He looked older, in some indefinable way, than when I'd last seen him. He'd shaved the beard, but kept his mustache—a rather luxuriant one. His dark hair was shorter than mine, now; almost an Establishment cut. He wore a suit and tie—a phenomenon unheard of since Exeter days.

"Hi." A sudden constraint had fallen upon me—a sense of the differences that had parted us slowly, inexorably, until an unbridgeable gap lay between us. We shared some memories, that was all; there was nothing in the present or the future that provided common ground on which we could meet.

"It's good to see you." The greenish-hazel eyes looked intently into mine as if he were aware of no gap.

"Same here. I was beginning to think it would never happen!"

"Tell me about my family. Mother and Julie—you've seen them?"

"Yes, of course." I started to reach into a pocket for Frances's letter, but he stopped me with a quick gesture.

"No, don't hand me anything—not now. Looks suspicious, exchanging envelopes or packages in a public park."

"My, you *are* careful!"

"Have to be. Second nature."

So I told him all the details I could remember of my several visits to Frances over the past two and a half years, and gave an account of my last meeting with Julie, when she'd brought the package for him to my apartment.

"Yeh, at least I can buy the magazine and read her travel pieces. She's pretty good. I've thought of writing her, but felt it might only make things worse. I did get in touch once—"

"They told me. About the coin collection."

"Yes. I needed money. But since then, huh-uh. Better if I stay out of their lives entirely—things being as they are."

"You're wrong," I told him. "Your mother is sick with worry over you. All the time. Not hearing from you couldn't possibly make the situation any better for her—only worse."

"But how can I write her? Or Julie either. From my permanent foxhole. Too risky, anyhow; I don't care so much about that on my own account, but for the others."

"So you *are* a member of an organized group . . ."

Warren's thin lips quirked in a smile. "You still apolitical, Lex? Or have you joined the hidebound ones like my uncle, who—"

I felt a surge of anger. "It's possible to be critical of the government, you know, without feeling you have to annihilate it. Anarchy is not—"

36

"Ah. I suppose you're for Hugo Praeger."

"Yes, as a matter of fact." I eyed him regretfully. "And if you hadn't so effectively exiled yourself from the scene in your own country, I think even you might have gone along with Praeger, now that he's making a bid for the presidency." I had often thought so, over the last couple of years, as Praeger had emerged, more and more, as the voice of America—younger America, anyhow. That the eminent newsman and publisher of *The New York Evening Standard* would form a third party and run next year I had no doubt.

Warren was frowning into the distance. "In any case it's too late for me to go home and join the voters. My commitments are in another direction."

"Are you sure? At least come home, and after you're cleared you can go on in your chosen course—whatever that is."

"Afraid not."

"Your uncle's discussed it with Murray Greenfield—you know his reputation, certainly—and says if you'll stand trial they'll get you off."

"No."

I sighed. "I told him you wouldn't come."

"Why were you so sure? . . . You believe I killed the state trooper?"

"No. I don't. It's just that—well, having gone underground with your revolutionary friends, you'll stick with them and their purposes, I assume, till you accomplish what you want to. Or fail to, unequivocally."

He looked amused. "You're arguing my side of the case very capably for me. I needn't say a word."

"Look, Warren. The important thing is—do you have proof that you didn't shoot the trooper? Proof that would have some weight in court?"

"No, I haven't."

"I suppose you're protecting Roy Lissing." Dislike for Roy shaded the words. "You should let him be responsible for his own crimes, not take blame that isn't yours."

"Maybe he didn't shoot Trooper Moore, either."

"He probably did and enjoyed it," I said stonily.

Warren was watching the squirrel, which had returned and was sitting in front of us, flirting its tail. "We'll get nowhere discussing this; as you can see."

"Well, I promised your uncle I'd give you the whole pitch."

"If we get around to it. I wouldn't be too scrupulous, if I were you, about doing whatever it is he wanted done. My uncle never in his life did anything that wasn't first and foremost for his own advantage. I doubt that he's eating his heart out because he wants to see me again—I'd have thought he'd feel he was well shut of me."

"Yes, I know. I was surprised—considering how you've trampled roughshod over his most cherished principles—that he spoke of you with such genuine feeling—"

"Suppressed rage. Of course."

"No. Affection. He connected it up, certainly, with his feelings about your father."

"Bad conscience, then. As long as my father lived, Uncle Oliver envied him every breath he drew. He *hated* being second son—you know that, Lex, you've seen it in a hundred ways. He couldn't bear it that Dad inherited the house they'd both grown up in; so that he was the one who had to move out—"

"He has it now. I suppose you'd heard that."

"Our house? Uncle Oliver lives there?" There was a quick contraction of his brows, and I wondered why I'd had to tell him. Bad enough to be an exile without learning that in your absence you'd been dispossessed of your boyhood home.

"Your mother didn't mention it, I guess, when she wrote you last year. She found the place too big and lonely, after you left. She's better off, really, in the Fifth Avenue apartment. And she still has the Palm Beach house. And Deer Head." Deer Head was one of the Thousand Islands, where the Thayers had always had a summer place. Not that I could see Frances going alone up to the wilds of the St. Lawrence.

"John is still with her," I went on. "Makes things seem somewhat as they were before."

He sighed. "Yes. Before."

"Tell me," I said. "What did you figure out about that message I got at first, to go to the Château?"

"Forget it. Forget the girl, too, and what she said. The whole thing was an attempt to scare both of us off from getting together. Well-meant, but needless."

"Friends of yours were responsible, then."

"Yes."

"I'm glad that's all it was. I felt for a while as if I were in the middle of a spy movie."

He smiled—but a little crookedly. And it came home to me how he must live all the time with tension, worry, the expectation of being arrested.

"Where do you live?"

"Oh, I have a small apartment. Not bad."

"You don't want to take me there?"

"No. Better not."

"You have a job? You look like a very proper businessman . . ." Though far from prosperous, I had noted. His tan suit verged on threadbare.

"Protective coloration. But I do have a job—I teach writing. Night classes and one on Saturday."

"What kind of students?"

"Every kind, though mostly the not-so-well-off. It's an adult self-improvement sort of thing. Kids, too—dropouts."

He'd hardly make much of a living doing that, I knew.

We had lunch at a cheap café—a dark little place where Warren seemed to feel at home. I was able, there, to pass his mother's letter to him, and the box containing the watch. He

39

put the box in his pocket and sat there reading the letter while we drank beer. There was money, too, in the letter—as I'd suspected from the feel of it. "Enough," he'd said as he put the bills in his wallet. "But not sufficient to dissuade me from coming home."

"So how do you feel about it now?" I asked as he finished reading and the omelets we had ordered arrived—slimy and gray-looking. "Want to try coming back, and clear up your problems via the law courts?"

"No." He put the long letter—sheets and sheets—in his pocket. "I can't, even if I wanted to. I have work to do here." There was a heaviness in his words, making me wonder whether the heart had gone out of his commitment to the group he was allied with. So that he stayed on simply because he was trapped in the movement?

"You still believe in what you're doing?"

"Oh, yes!" Such a positive response that I knew he had not changed his mind about things, as Uncle Oliver had hoped.

We sat till midafternoon in the café, just talking. Then he walked back with me toward my hotel.

"I'll leave you here," he said when we were still a couple of blocks from the Genève. "What're your plans now?" We had stopped in the shade of a large tree that overhung the sidewalk.

"If I thought I could change your mind, I'd stay on longer in Montreal."

"I won't change my mind. It's been great talking to you, catching up on so many things that have happened. What's rough—the only thing I really mind—about my present life is having to give up my family, my old friends; not just temporarily, but for good. Today's been a freak—time borrowed from the past—being able to talk to you. Such a thing can't happen to me again."

He reached out and grasped my shoulder. "Take care." His hand dropped.

40

"Any word for your mother?"

"I'll write her. This time, anyway." He started to turn away.

"Badger, this is insane! You can't throw your life away, give up—"

He smiled. "Oh, but I can! And it's not thrown away. If you knew what I'm trying to accomplish just now, I think you'd approve."

And with that enigmatic remark he raised his hand in farewell and walked away, back in the direction from which we had come. I watched him. Watched until he disappeared from view, taking with him a part of me that would be now lost; who but Warren Thayer knew or would remember the things that had been so important to a boy named Alex Norden fifteen years ago . . . eighteen years . . . twelve? Memories, with no one to share them, are lonely.

Yet Warren's most of all, I thought; when he had turned his back on all his past.

Was this really the last I would ever see of him?

4

It was late to try to leave the city that day. Better to wait till tomorrow and then decide what to do.

I think you'd approve? What in the world was Warren doing that I'd approve of? Scratch any idea that his whole activist career was a fake! There *were* people who surfaced now and then in the news, claiming to have been undercover government agents who had infiltrated some revolutionary group or another. But Warren was not conceivably one of those. I had watched the evolution of his beliefs from too far back even to consider that he could be anything but dedicated to the principles he had served now for so long.

I phoned Oliver Thayer to tell him it was all over. The meeting, the refusal to come back to the States.

"I see. Yes. I'm extremely disappointed, Alex. And this will be still another blow to Frances. She was counting—"

"Yes, I know."

"What about this man who was following you the other day? Did—"

I gave him Warren's explanation. "But I had checked out of the hotel, in any case, and taken care not to leave a trail."

"So that's it! I wondered. I tried to get in touch with you

42

today at the Queen Elizabeth and learned you weren't there any more. Where *are* you now? In case—"

"Oh, it's a little place in the old part of town. L'Hôtel Genève. Though it doesn't matter now. I doubt that I'll be here much longer."

"You think there's not much chance, then, that he'll change his mind . . ."

"No chance at all."

"Well, thanks, anyway. I appreciate all you've done, Alex— appreciate it more than I can say."

So that was that.

Twenty minutes later my phone rang.

"I'm sorry it didn't work." It was Julie Thayer.

"So am I, Julie. I gather your father told you."

"Yes. He just now called. Want to take me to dinner?"

"You're here? In Montreal?" I was sure there had been only a fractional pause while I figured that out.

"I flew up last night, after we heard from Daddy that you'd been in touch with Warren. How is he?" There was a catch in her voice.

"He's fine. Just won't leave what he's doing, that's all."

"You don't know where he lives?"

"No."

"Or how I could reach him somewhere else?"

"No way, Julie."

"If you say so."

"I'd love to take you to dinner."

She had suggested we go somewhere relaxed—and was dressed accordingly, looking very beautiful in a softly draped dress and jacket of lavender-blue. I picked her up at the Queen Elizabeth. She'd registered there because she had thought that was where I was.

She suggested a couple of restaurants, and I decided which

43

one. Restaurants in any city of the world were the kind of thing she knew from her travel job.

The place looked like a wine cellar, with bottles racked in tiers against the rough stone walls. The warm smell of garlic, a promise of solid French cooking, enfolded us as we entered.

We were seated in a corner, at a table with fresh flowers and a yellow cloth.

"Tell me all about him . . ." she said.

I did. While she drank white wine and I had Scotch.

All our lives, she'd had the knack of invariably putting me at a disadvantage; maybe she didn't do it consciously, though I'd often doubted that. Many a time I'd had the thought that she wanted nothing so much as to have my neck under her heel.

None of that this evening. Perhaps, I guessed, she was not even aware of me; only of Warren and his problems.

When I'd finished my play-by-play description of the day, she sat for a minute or so just staring into space. "Well, no one can ever change him," she said finally.

"No."

Her eyes came back to meet mine as if she'd only now remembered I was there. "Did he like the watch?"

"I gave him the box, but he didn't open it."

"Oh." She was disappointed not to have his reaction.

"He said something about its looking suspicious to exchange packages or envelopes in a public place, so I slipped it to him under the table at lunch."

She gave a wry grin. "I guess in the circles he moves in—"

It was a marvelous restaurant. Escargots predictably redolent of garlic, crusty French bread. I had cold salmon, and Julie ordered bass.

"About the café where you had lunch," she said abruptly, breaking off from something she'd been telling me about the last time she'd come to Montreal. "From what you said, it sounded as if it might be a regular place of Warren's."

I thought about that. "It may be."

44

Her face lit up. "If you take me there tomorrow, maybe we'll run into him."

"He wouldn't want you trying that, I'm sure. He was worried enough about *me* being trailed by police, in hopes they would net him. But *you*—when you're actually related . . ."

I expected a sharp answer, and she started to give me one, but the combative glow faded in her eyes, leaving only a look of realistic appraisal.

"Then we'll lay a false trail. Just as you did."

It took her a while, but she talked me into it.

Probably no risk to Warren in any case—chances were he wouldn't go back for a month to the café where we'd eaten.

She seemed cheered because we'd at least made some kind of plan.

And so was I. Not that I thought she could sway Warren in a matter about which he clearly was adamant. If we even ran into him tomorrow. Or the next day. Or the day after that.

I walked back to my hotel, after I'd said good night to Julie in the lobby of the Queen Elizabeth, and as I strode along the evening streets—cooler now—found that I was looking forward to tomorrow with more anticipation than there seemed any reason for.

It was a long way from Dorchester Boulevard, in the heart of the modern city, to Vieux Montrèal, where the Genève was located. There was little traffic on the streets, but people still wandered along the sidewalks here and there. Though when I arrived at Place Jacques Cartier, with its string of cafés, it was jammed with people, most of them student age. A completely different world, this, from the expensive-hotel-and-chic-restaurant area I had left.

I reached the Hôtel Genève, on its corner across from a little stone church and next to a tumble-down brick building that looked like a warehouse.

As I passed through the hotel's small seedy lobby—no more than a hallway, really—I walked of necessity not two feet from the registration desk. Almost without thinking, I scanned the grid of numbered boxes behind it, and I saw that there was a message for me.

The desk clerk—an elderly, watery-eyed little man—handed it to me.

It was a telephone message. Filled in on a form. Mr. Doe had called. At 9:40 P.M.

Hope you can have breakfast with me. About 9:00.

Warren, of course.

Had he changed his mind?

Breakfast where? Presumably he'd phone in the morning to tell me where to meet him.

But I didn't call Julie to let her know. I'd find out first what had moved Warren to get in touch with me again.

At ten of nine the next morning the sudden harsh ring of the room phone jolted me like an electric shock. I'd been up since early, ready for Warren's call, and the waiting had strung up my nerves.

"Mr. Doe is here to see you." A male voice with a French accent.

Surprise outweighed any other reaction—I'd assumed he'd phone from somewhere and tell me where to meet him.

"Have him come up." Even before I put down the phone, I felt the sudden chill one gets upon receipt of bad news. The bad news being that last night I'd taken no precautions against being followed here from the Queen Elizabeth. No reason to. And now Warren was downstairs . . .

Surely no one had been following me—at any time? Or following Julie either? Last night—

I moved to the door and opened it. My room was on the third floor, on a small hall that intersected the main one. It would take Warren only moments to come up the stairs. I left my door

46

open and crossed to the main corridor.

He was just coming to the top of the stairs. He emerged, looked left and right, and I called out to him.

"Warren!"

He was silhouetted against a window at the front of the hotel. I saw him walk quickly toward me. It was then that the report came, deafeningly loud, spreading through the hall and down the stairwell to the lobby.

Warren stumbled.

I remember running forward, slowly as in a bad dream, reaching him as he fell.

As I struggled, with my arm around his ribs, to get him to his knees, then to his feet, I was aware that we were quite alone in the corridor.

His legs weren't quite useless, and together we made it to my room. I closed and bolted the door and let him down onto the bed.

He was hit in the right shoulder. I eased him to a sitting position and got his jacket off; tore away the shirt from the area around the wound. Blood welled up from an ugly hole.

"I've got to get out of here." He was hunched up, head bent, and I barely heard him.

"Not in this condition." I wadded up the piece of shirt I'd torn away and stuck it against the wound. "Press here." I crossed the room to the washbasin—a luxury, at that, in the kind of hotel where the bath was down the hall.

Years since I'd had some kind of rudimentary first-aid course. I managed to get him cleaned up, and bound some padding, including a clean washcloth and a hand towel, over the hole.

"Do you know who did this?" I asked as I tore strips from a sheet.

"No."

"Any guesses?"

"Maybe."

47

I wound the strips around him, length after length. The third-floor hall was no longer empty. We could hear a babble of voices.

"Keep pressing on this," I told him. "Or you'll bleed all over the place."

"I've *got* to get out of here! They'll have called the police—listen to them!" One thing we did know, at least, was that it couldn't have been anyone connected with the law who had taken the shot at him; police don't fire and run away—they close in.

"Where can we go?" I asked.

"My place."

"You'll never make it."

"We'll get a taxi. Is there a fire escape?" He nodded toward the windows.

"Yes. One piece of luck, anyhow—" My room was on the corner at the back of the hotel, where a fire escape crisscrossed the brick wall of the building and led down into an alley.

I got one of my shirts onto him—took some doing, with the bandages—and warned him against moving his arm for fear he'd worsen the bleeding. "You'd better have a sling," I suggested.

I got a cardigan sweater on over the shirt—the better to conceal the padding. Then rigged a sling and fixed his arm in it. He kept telling me to hurry.

Voices had grown louder in the hall, and by the time we climbed out the rear window, someone was knocking on my door.

Word of the excitement in the hotel hadn't yet leaked out to the neighborhood; so far, anyway, the windows of the buildings opposite, across the alley, seemed free of onlookers.

The last segment of the fire escape was the kind that swings up when not in use. It was already down. I had time to wonder fleetingly whether it had just been used as an exit by someone else.

48

Warren clung to the iron railings, on the way down, and I helped him as best I could. By the last flight he was almost a dead weight for me to drag along.

"You going to pass out?" I asked.

"Don't know," he said thickly. "Try not to."

"A taxi's no good." We had reached the bottom step. I helped him set foot on the concrete, took him a couple of steps and braced him against the brick wall of the hotel. I pulled up on the set of iron stairs, pushed, and the whole section swung up against the second-floor fire escape where it belonged. "Police'll trace us if we go by taxi. Assuming we can even find one that'll take us. I'll get my car from the parking lot. It's not too far—"

"Afraid—I can't walk—" His skin was greenish pale, and I knew he couldn't make it any distance.

"We'll walk far enough to get out of sight of the hotel. I'll stash you in some car parked at the curb till I come back."

He nodded, but said nothing.

We hobbled as far as the entrance to our alley, and I propped him up again. Looked out. I saw no police. But an approaching siren sounded over the noise of nearby traffic. Not much time.

We made our way painstakingly to the next cross street behind the hotel. I was afraid we wouldn't even manage that much, but at last we turned the corner. I tried the door of the second car in, one of a long line parked at the curb. It was locked.

Tried the next one. Locked. And the police siren died away behind us, right by the hotel.

The next car was unlocked. I put Warren into the back seat.

"Scoot over to the other side; I'll fish you out from there. I'll be as quick as I can. If the owner of the car comes back, you've made a mistake, it—"

"I'll manage." Or I think that's what he said.

I closed the door on him, and sweating from the effort of

getting Warren this far when he could hardly stand or move, I took off.

Two blocks to the parking lot. Luckily the ticket was in my wallet, not lying back in my room on the dresser.

The attendant, when I got there, was arguing with someone in French, and paid no attention to me.

"Vite, vite!" I said, and added, *"S'il vous plait. Je suis en retard—"*

The swarthy face with a forehead full of black curly hair under a dirty cap turned to me. *"Oui—oui. Tout de suit."*

But it was not *tout de suit.* He argued for an age with his paunchy companion—an acquaintance, I thought, not a customer. At last he took my ticket, computed what I owed and took my money. He had to move only two cars to get mine out.

In more of a sweat than ever, and my teeth bared in impatience, I pulled out into the street. Had to go a long way round to get back to Warren, because of a one-way street.

Finally. Two blocks from the Genève I turned into the street down which we had struggled. Only a block to go to the intersection where I'd left Warren. The traffic inched along, stopped. I could see what the trouble was: a police car, with its lights flashing, was pulled up beside the hotel, partially blocking the street.

Not much time to get clear of the area. I inched along behind the car ahead. Made a little progress; was stopped again.

They'd find the bloody towels in my room, and would know which way we'd gone—down the fire escape. Any minute now the police would come tearing out of that alley in pursuit.

Made a little more progress.

And then I was turning into the street, double-parking beside the dark red Buick.

He wasn't there. No one in the car, I saw as I got out on the passenger side of mine.

I peered through the window and there he was, lying on the seat. I wrenched the door open.

"Come on."

He didn't answer.

I leaned in. Shook him. Gently at first, and then harder. Because it is almost impossible to get an inert body out of the back seat of a car; there's no way to get leverage.

He groaned, and his eyes flickered open.

"Come on, Warren. No time to lose."

He raised himself enough that I could grab hold of him and pull him to a sitting position. "Come on, now. Get out of the car."

It was an incredible struggle, and there was no use paying any attention to whether passers-by were looking our way. At last he pulled himself into my car and I closed the door on him.

A girl was standing on the curb, absorbed in our little drama. I smiled at her, shrugged, and shook my head, with—I hoped —an air that suggested "Drunk again!" Got in and drove off.

"Which way am I to go?"

"Straight ahead, for now."

"Still heading for your place? We'd better get you to a doctor—"

"No. Not now, anyway."

"Yes. That bullet's smashed up a lot in there—"

"Didn't touch my lungs—that's what matters." His speech was fuzzy, but he seemed to have revived a little.

"How do you know it didn't?"

"I'd know. Bloody froth or something."

"Hell, you're no doctor!"

"Well, never mind. You didn't see anyone, Lex? In the hall, on the stairs—?"

"Not a soul. Either he shot from the stairwell, or from one of the rooms—and then closed the door. I'd guess that he left by the fire escape, while I was dressing your shoulder—the last flight of steps had been lowered before we got there."

"Pity we didn't look out the window."

51

"Good thing he didn't look in."

"Turn soon, now. Next traffic signal. Turn left."

"Listen," I said when we had turned. "Julie's in town." There hadn't been even a moment when I could have told him —too many urgent matters to attend to.

The news might help to keep him conscious, too, I thought —I didn't want him falling asleep on me.

"Julie! Oh, no! Don't need her in the middle of all this—"

"Well, she isn't. How could she be? She'll be waiting for me to pick her up, very shortly now, at the Queen Elizabeth. So we can go and look for you." I told him about her calling me the afternoon before, and our going to dinner.

"You didn't call her after you had my message last night?"

"No. Thought it wiser to wait and see what was on your mind."

He didn't answer. Didn't feel up to making the effort, probably.

"But *why*," I asked, "did you take such a risk as to come to my hotel? You could have phoned—I could have met you. Could have taken precautions—"

"Didn't seem to be any reason for precautions," he said faintly. "I thought the Genève was a safe place—after all your dodging and laying of false trails before you took up residence there."

"But still—"

"How was I to know you'd been seen all over town last night with Julie? By anyone who was looking?"

Yes. How could he have known—

I drove carefully. Didn't want to be picked up, at this point, for a traffic violation.

I wondered how long it would be before my license number would be on the police band.

5

Warren lived in an old brick building that even in better days couldn't have looked like much. There were others like it all along the street—some with stores in the ground floor. His was purely residential—four stories, with a coping of cast concrete made to look like stone, and insets of the same all over the face of the brick, giving the building a blotched appearance.

We'd argued the matter of a doctor or a hospital, and I'd lost. He was heading home to hole up.

I double-parked in front.

"You going to be able to make it to the door?"

"With a little help. Sure."

I got out and came around the car. He was easing out, holding onto the door and the seat back. I grasped him, with an arm around his waist, and together we made it across the sidewalk and up three steps to the building's dingy entrance. Whether anyone had taken particular interest in our progress in tandem, I didn't know.

Warren leaned against the wall of the narrow entry. "Haywood," he said, repeating the name he'd given me during the ride here; I saw it, W. R. Haywood, the name cut from a printed card and stuck in the slot by a bellpush—one of a row in front of me on the wall. His apartment was number eight.

"I'll go on up." He pushed open the glass door to the hall beyond. "Lock broken," he said. Holding onto the door, he edged in.

"Be back as soon as I can." I had to find someplace to put the car—and not too near; eventually the police would have my license number. If they didn't now. They might not know exactly what it was that had happened, back at the hotel (nor did I), but after finding the bloody record of Warren's brief stay in my room, they would be bending every effort to find out.

I drove quite a distance before parking, and walked back.

No sign of Warren in the lower hall or on the stairway—thank God no blood dripped on the linoleum treads, either. I went up the stairs and along the second-floor hall to the back.

The door of number eight was slightly ajar.

I went in and closed it behind me.

He lay on a double bed that stood against the right-hand wall. His face was still that white color, with a greenish cast.

"We've got to get you to a doctor," I started in again.

"No. Not here. Roy will find me one."

"Then where do I get hold of Roy?"

"You don't." His eyes closed. "If you'll just stay with me till Eve comes—in case I black out. I don't want to black out when no one's here. Silly as that may sound." There was the suggestion of a smile at the corners of his lips.

"Eve?" I asked.

Without opening his eyes, he made a gesture that included the room. "Eve."

I hadn't even looked at the room. I glanced around, now, at an environment created almost wholly by illusion. The walls were chalk-white, and on them were painted blue shutters, at the windows—wildly romantic Mediterranean shutters, like something from a backdrop at the Met. A seascape was depicted on the wall to the left—framed by a sketched-in window on whose sill slept a tawny two-dimensional cat, its tail dan-

54

gling just over a scarred old table which was real and which had been lacquered blue. The simulated wrought-iron headboard of the bed of course existed only on the wall.

"Very talented," I said. "Extraordinarily." The things had been done with a wonderful flair; none of the awkwardness of an amateur about their execution.

Warren had not answered.

"But when will she come?"

"Anytime. I don't know."

"You're sure she *will* come?"

"She lives here." He patted the other side of the bed with his hand.

"Can I reach her somewhere?"

"No," he whispered.

I checked the bandage I'd put on him. There had been some bleeding, but it seemed to have stopped. I argued with him again: this was definitely the time to give himself up . . . It was the only course open to him, in fact; only way he'd get the immediate medical care he must have.

He listened and said no.

"But hadn't you changed your mind, Warren, after all? I thought that must have been the reason you were coming to see me this morning—"

"Not the reason."

"Why did you come, then?"

He opened his eyes and looked at me, but said nothing. He must have been too drained of strength even to attempt to tell me. The fingers of his left hand lifted, and dropped, in a dismissing gesture, and he closed his eyes again.

It was nearly eleven, I saw.

I was to have picked Julie up twenty minutes ago. We wouldn't have the day together now; the pang of loss struck me even in the midst of my concern for Warren.

Julie would shrug off my nonappearance, no doubt, as simply a change of mind about taking her with me.

55

We waited. I wondered when the girl named Eve would be coming.

He seemed to have fallen asleep.

There was no phone in the room. I thought of going out and finding one; call an ambulance and have them fetch him away before he knew what had happened. But one doesn't do such a thing to a friend. Not even to save his life.

I wandered about his quarters. There was the one large room, off it a bathroom and a tiny kitchen in an alcove. No closet, but an old armoire, antiqued and painted a soft green.

No posters, here, of Che Guevara. But the books in the rickety bookcase left no doubt of their owner's political leanings.

I began to wonder whether he might simply die, lying there. Lapse into a coma. I leaned over him and watched his breathing.

There were footsteps in the hall. As I straightened up from bending over the bed, a key grated in the lock. The door opened.

She was not very tall; a girl with short sandy hair, and with great dark eyes, set in an enchanting face that looked for some reason childish—though she was clearly not a child. She stopped short when she saw me, and then her glance fell to Warren on the bed.

She did not move for just that moment in which she realized and adjusted to the fact that something was wrong. Her eyes lifted to mine again and she said accusingly, "What's the matter with him?"

It was not until she spoke that I recognized her as the girl who had accosted me in the street on the day of the Château de Ramezay episode. Her appearance was completely different without the makeup, the scarf that had covered her light hair, and the corny earrings.

"He's been shot," I said.

Her eyes widened and her lips parted. She brushed past me. "Warren! Warren—"

His eyes opened.

"How bad?" she asked.

"I don't know," I told her. "It's in his shoulder."

"Hi," Warren contributed, looking up at the girl.

"How bad?" she repeated.

"Well, I walked away from the scene of the crime—"

"Hardly unassisted," I pointed out. "Look—Eve? We've got to get him to a doctor."

She was inspecting his bandages, trying to figure out exactly where the wound was. "I'll go and call Roy. He'll know what to do." She grabbed up the shoulderbag she'd dropped on the floor and was gone.

But I wondered where Roy Lissing was going to get hold of a doctor—one who would treat a man for a bullet wound and not report it to the police.

"We're to sit tight," she said when she came back. "And you'll stay, won't you?" she asked me. "We're going to have to move him, and we'll need you."

"You don't think I'd walk out on him at this point, do you?" I said with probably needless heat.

"I should hope not! Seeing as this is all your fault."

"How is it my fault?" Though I'd already told myself it was; if I'd never come here to look for him—

"Did you see who it was who shot you?" she asked of the still form between us, and Warren gently shook his head. "Either of you? Where did it happen?"

I told her, and she fixed me with her accusing glance again. "If you can't make a good guess at who's behind this, you're more stupid than Warren tells me you are. It was Uncle Oliver —who else! Why do you think he sent you here? *He* doesn't want any member of the Thayer family dragged back to New

York and tried—think of the publicity! Him and his family pride . . . He had only one thing in mind, dear Alex, when he dispatched you up here to find your old buddy. He sent you to ferret him out so he could be killed. . . ."

I tried to deny to myself that what she said could be true. Early in this undertaking I had wondered whether I might be a Judas goat; the thought had crossed my mind, at least—but I'd discarded it. Now?

"Men like Oliver Thayer don't shoot people."

"Not personally—of course not." She was sitting on the edge of the bed, holding Warren's hand. "They have it done."

"By whom?" I argued. "A man in Oliver Thayer's position couldn't afford to have someone like that hanging around afterward—a hit man who could blackmail him?"

"I'm sure he could manage. Use a nobody—and later when something happens to the nobody, who's to connect an inconspicuous murder, or supposed accident, with a top-ranking socialite millionaire?"

Warren seemed to get no worse; he slept most of the time. Eve heated some canned soup and we ate it with crackers and some milk. And while we waited, she gathered a few articles of clothing together—hers and Warren's—and put them in a small suitcase she dragged out from under the bed.

I watched her moving about, hovering over Warren. It was the roundness of her eyes, and the way they were set, that gave her face a suggestion of childishness, I decided. The way she looked at Warren was mature enough.

It was almost two hours before Roy Lissing came.

Eve let him in. Except for his build—tall, lanky, stooped— I'd have had difficulty recognizing him. He'd grown a beard, which hid the receding chin I remembered as one of his identifying features. His pale eyes, though, were the same—filled with dislike, and gleaming now with self-righteous malice.

"Proud of what you've accomplished here?" he said to me. "Got your friend shot, I understand."

My teeth clenched hard together. "Listen—I'm not responsible in any—"

The pale eyes raked me. "You're not responsible. Period." He moved over to the bed. "How's it going, Warren?"

"Not bad. Think I could do with some repair work, though." For the first time there was a hint of apprehension in his face as he looked up at Lissing. Now that there was some kind of help in the offing—presumably—he needn't try so hard to keep up a stoic front.

"We'll manage something." Lissing gave him a confident smile. "We'll get you out—" he threw a side glance at me— "well, you know where. Take you there first, then we'll see."

"You sound a little vague," I challenged him, "as to how soon he's going to get some medical attention. It's already been hours—"

Roy Lissing's mouth twisted to one side—an ugly hole in his beard. "You don't have a vote in this outfit, Norden. We're doing the best we can within the limits of quite difficult circumstances. Now you going to shut up and help?"

I shut up and helped. We got Warren down the stairs and into the back of a panel truck, bedded down on a couple of blankets. Lissing and I sat on the floor, on either side of him, while Eve drove.

"You're not to look out," Lissing instructed me.

"Can't see a thing from here, don't worry." I sat facing the rear, my back against the driver's seat. There were no windows in the sides or in the double back doors.

I tried to keep track of our direction, but when we got onto one of the superhighways it was difficult to determine anything —the network of new limited-access roads wound like a mass of spaghetti over the surface of the city, and a long, slow curve could put you onto a route going almost anywhere. I'd time the trip at least; I sneaked a look at my watch. A quarter of two. God! Five hours, just about, since he'd been shot.

We got to where we were going after about an hour and a half. The back doors of the panel truck were opened by a young man with shoulder-length blond hair, and rippling muscles under his tan. He greeted Warren with affection and dismay. "Hey! What happened to you!" He stepped up into the truck and knelt beside him.

"Hi, Mick. Guess I'm kind of a mess."

I climbed out of the truck and discovered that we were parked at the side door of a farmhouse. A disheveled-looking place, the house sided with greenish-black asphalt shingles. There were an unpainted barn and a shed with only a back wall to it, across the rutted drive from the house. Some farm equipment rusted in tall weeds beside the barn, which stood at the bottom of a steep pine-clad slope. Behind the house was a large well-tended vegetable garden, and beyond it empty fields. In front of the house, extending toward the road, was a pasture containing some sheep. In the middle distance on two sides of us were high hills.

"This is Warren's friend," Roy stated succinctly to Mick. The introduction went unacknowledged, but Mick and I together got Warren into the house. We went through the kitchen and into a room behind it which seemed to be some kind of storeroom. There were some cartons on the floor, and under the window an old iron-framed folding bed was made up with sheets and a blanket.

"How you feel?" Roy Lissing hung over Warren when we'd laid him down. Mick hovered at the foot of the bed, looking upset.

"Not too bad." Warren tried for a smile, but it wasn't much of a success.

Eve pushed past the others to take a place by the patient. She felt his forehead. "Roy—he's running a fever."

"What happened to Warren?" A female voice behind me. I turned to see at my elbow a girl of about twenty-five, with long brown hair done in a twist on top of her head. She was dressed in jeans and a man's shirt, and carried a basket of tomatoes.

It was Roy who explained to her what had happened to Warren.

"Do we have any kind of access to a doctor?" Mick asked anxiously—of no one in particular.

"You know we don't!" the girl answered.

"Nurse?" Mick again, but even more doubtfully.

Roy Lissing turned to the girl. "Where's Gary?"

"In the workroom."

"Go get him."

She vanished, and we waited, with Eve checking Warren's bandages and shaking her head.

I turned as I heard someone crossing the kitchen behind me. A fat boy, with three chins and button eyes, and a lock of dark, lank hair falling over his forehead, came into the room, behind him the girl, still carrying the tomatoes, which she'd apparently forgotten she had.

Roy motioned Gary over to the bedside. "Take a look at our casualty, here."

"Tough shit," said Gary. "I hear they winged you."

"A little worse than that," Roy corrected him. "He's got a bullet in the shoulder."

Gary pushed back the hair that hung in his face. "Where we gonna get him a doctor, Roy?"

"I'm afraid *you're* the doctor, Gary."

Gary's mouth fell open as he stared at Roy Lissing, and Eve slewed around to look up at him—incredulous.

"Roy! *He's* not a trained physician—he knows nothing about—"

"He studied to be a vet, didn't he?"

"Christ, I never *got* to vet school even. I dropped out before that."

61

"You told me you'd had comparative anatomy as an under-graduate." Roy looked at him steadily. "Dissected a cat, you said—"

"A cat, yes!" Gary's little dark button eyes were filled with horror. "That's not the same as—"

"And you assisted at a vet hospital all one summer. Watched them operate, you told me."

"Oh, but, Roy—"

"Roy, you can't!" said Eve, appalled at what he was propos-ing. (Well, so was I!) She took him urgently by the arm. "War-ren could *die!* We've got to have a doctor—a real one. We can kidnap one; bring him here blindfolded. I'll go myself, and Mick—and Lucia." She appealed to the other girl. "Lucia, you'll go, won't you? With three of us—"

"No," Roy said quietly. "It's too risky. Once any doctor's had a look at the famous fugitive Thayer, and at the setup here, it'll be no time at all before the Royal Canadian Mounties are crawling all over this place."

"He's right," Warren said quietly.

"You see?" Roy looked around at those assembled. "Gary, you're elected."

"I can't. I don't know how. I can't possibly—"

Roy turned on him angrily. "For God's sake, man, what do you think they did in the Old West when somebody got a bullet in 'im? They probed for it and they got it out. You've seen it a dozen times on *Gunsmoke*—it's not that difficult."

"*You* do it, then."

"No. You know more about it than I do; you've dissected a cat."

"I'm game if you are, Gary." Warren spoke with eyes still shut.

"A cat! My God!" said Eve. Tears stood in her eyes, and for a moment she looked my way in appeal. I wished again that I'd been able to convince Warren, way back this morning, to give himself up. The only plan that came to mind was the possibility

62

of kidnapping him, myself, if this fat college dropout botched things and Warren's condition worsened. If it came down to a real likelihood of his dying . . .

Eve was dispatched—objecting, because she wanted to stay with Warren—to the nearest village to buy sterile cotton, gauze, adhesive tape and disinfectant.

"Best for you to go," Roy told her. "The natives know us by sight, and we don't want them wondering why we need this stuff. They'll think you're just a tourist, some camper passing through. So don't park the truck in front of the drugstore."

The patient was given a few good slugs of rum—the only alcohol they seemed to have on hand besides some wine—to ready him for the ordeal. Lucia scrubbed up the white enamel table in the kitchen, according to Gary's instructions, and boiled some instruments—an icepick, a sharp kitchen knife, a pair of tweezers, scissors, a stainless steel needle, two knitting needles—one metal, one plastic.

As soon as Eve came back, we started. There were just Gary, Eve and me around the table, with dishtowels tied over our faces for surgical masks. Everyone scrubbed up. Eve scrubbed up the patient, and she and I held him. The other three watched from a distance.

"Where'd you get the fancy timepiece?" Roy had suddenly noticed it.

I answered for Warren. "His sister sent it to him. I brought it."

"Farewell gift from the family," I heard Roy murmur.

Gary began—probing with the green plastic knitting needle. He worked tentatively, seemingly afraid to go very deep. Even with his gingerly prodding, the blood began to well up again in the wound, and Eve had to blot it away with sterile cotton.

"You don't seem to be getting anywhere," she remarked causticly.

"Have to be careful. Could hit an artery." Perspiration stood on his forehead.

63

"Oh," she said. "Great."

Gary was gazing hopelessly at the ugly hole and the mess he was making of it. His hands shook. Eve looked like death, herself, the color gone from her face, the round, childish eyes fear-haunted. At this point, any other course of action but the one they were on would have tremendous appeal. I offered them one.

"I suggest we bandage him up again and you let me take him to a hospital. He'll be giving himself up, but his uncle's guaranteed us he'll be acquitted when he comes to trial. And surely he can do you-all as much good operating in the open again as he can bottled up here? Certainly he's more good alive than dead—"

"No. How stupid can you get, Norden!" Roy spoke from behind me, where he leaned in the outside doorway watching. "He'd never live to come to trial! Haven't you figured out yet who shot him? Had him shot, anyhow. Not the police—they'd have taken him into custody on the spot. So who else is there? No one but Oliver Thayer; there's no one else who would want him dead. No one else, either, who knew where to find him this morning—courtesy of you.

"So we're not handing him over to due process—and another assassination attempt."

Gary, during this harangue, was looking sicker and sicker. He wiped his forehead with the back of his wrist. His mouth opened, like that of a fish. Abruptly he said, "I think I'm going to faint . . ."

I took the knitting needle from his hand and he turned away and fled from the room.

"Can you do it?" Eve asked, her voice husky.

"I'll try. No choice, is there? Roy, get over here and help to hold him."

No use giving a play-by-play account of my one and only surgical performance. It was frustrating, scary, at times seemed impossible of success. I thought I had the bullet, and came up with a bone fragment. And I can say definitely that a pair of ordinary tweezers does not have the reach to fish out something that has been imbedded with the force supplied by a .32 handgun. (I could only guess at the caliber then, but that was what it had been.)

I got it out—with some desperate last-minute assistance from Eve.

I had no intention of sewing the wound shut; didn't know how. Instead I closed it up with a number of Band-Aids, then put sterile gauze and adhesive tape over the whole thing, having no idea what kind of germ-infested mess I'd left inside.

"Have you got any antibiotics?" I asked.

"That's the next thing on the list," Roy answered. We were helping Warren down off the table; he was breathing harshly and deeply, as he had during the last of the operation, to help cope with the pain. He was limp as a dead rabbit as we lifted him down. Mick, who'd been waiting out of the way in the storeroom door, came into the kitchen. He and Roy made a chair with their hands, and got Warren back to his bed.

"Thanks," he said to me, his eyes half-closed. "You missed your calling." Almost a whisper. Eve was fussing around him and he seemed to drop right off to sleep.

The rest of us went back to the kitchen, where Lucia was washing up the implements in the old brown-stained sink. The bullet lay on the drainboard on a piece of Kleenex. I picked it up.

Roy put out his hand. "I'll take that."

"No. I'll keep it. If there's ever a chance of proving who shot him, it won't come *your* way. Only a police lab is set up to compare this bullet with another. I can't see you trotting around to the authorities to ask them about it . . ."

"You mean you're not gonna close ranks with Uncle Oliver and the rest of the Thayers and pretend this little shooting never happened?"

"I don't give a damn about Uncle Oliver. Unless he did plan

this—in which case I hope they restore capital punishment." I put the little piece of lead, wrapped in the Kleenex, into my shirt pocket. "So where are you going to get him some antibiotics?"

"I'll get some. Don't worry. I'll be leaving soon for just that purpose."

"The sooner the better."

"I quite agree. Because of technical difficulties, it can't be just yet."

I thought I knew what the difficulties were. He was going to have to break into a pharmacy somewhere. And in order for him to break in, he had to wait first for it to close.

I had known, really, that I was their prisoner—from the moment Roy Lissing had arrived at Warren's apartment in Montreal. I could have walked out on them at that point—they couldn't have stopped me. But to take off then would have been running out on Warren. I couldn't have done that.

Nothing was said, as the afternoon ground on to its conclusion, to clarify my status, but I noticed a silent signal passed now and again from Roy to Gary or Mick—a little inclination of the head in my direction, as he himself went to check on the patient in the store-room, or stepped out the side door of the kitchen into the yard. Someone was to keep an eye on me at all times.

Lucia cooked dinner and we ate it at the white enamel table. There was no meat. Zucchini casserole, green beans, and sliced tomatoes. A very good peach cobbler for dessert.

Eve ate her dinner in the storeroom with Warren. When I went in to see him, after I'd finished my cobbler, he was asleep.

"He didn't eat . . . He had some tea, was all." I thought she was trying not to sound worried.

"He probably wouldn't eat much, at this stage. I wish we had the antibiotics—"

"Roy'll be going soon."

66

"Has to wait till it's dark, I presume."

"That's right. I wish it wasn't taking so long."

Roy came into the room. "I'm going."

"Who're you taking with you?"

"Lucia." He turned his attention to me. "You are in the nature of a spy," he said. "For that reason you're to be restricted to this room and the kitchen. And the john, of course, but that's right off the kitchen. Understood?"

"It was pretty clear without your mentioning it."

"Well, good. And just because we've been rather casual about having you around all day, don't think you can up and leave if the mood strikes you. Make one move to bust out of here and Mick or one of the rest of us will shoot you without a second thought and plunk you right under the compost heap where you'll do the most good." He winked—coldly—and I thought he would be delighted to see me dead right now.

I watched his hunched, narrow shoulders as he disappeared into the kitchen. "I'll stay with Warren," I told Eve. "You need a break for a while."

She nodded and left us, and I heard her running water in the bathroom. Out in the yard, the panel truck started up and was driven away.

Warren opened his eyes. "I shouldn't have let you come along."

I smiled. "You couldn't have prevented me."

"I wasn't thinking—I guess my mind was fogged up or I'd have told you to run like hell before Roy ever got there. Once Eve was with me, I could have—"

"Don't fret. I knew what I was getting into and I'm glad I came."

He snorted. "Oh, you couldn't be!"

"How do you feel?" I changed the subject.

"Not bad." He grinned. "Remember when I broke my arm falling out of the maple tree? This isn't any worse."

Mick and Gary came in to see how he was doing. I moved

aside, out of their way. And though I was the one who was Warren Thayer's old friend, the obvious closeness of the three of them made me an outsider.

I was reminded of what my father had tried to tell me about friendships in World War II. For Warren's group, dissidence was their war; like and unlike, it had united them.

Eve came back in a little while and tried to shoo us out.

"He needs peace and quiet, for Christ's sake!"

"Lex can stay—" Warren pleaded. "Who knows when I'll see him again after this?"

So I remained, along with Eve.

"You're not to talk," she told him. She sat beside him on an old dining-room chair—a rickety thing with a threadbare blue-upholstered seat.

"I can listen—" he said, and closed his eyes.

We talked for a little—very low. Just Eve and I.

"Why," I asked, "did you go through all that business of the letter, and meeting me in a disguise, the other day? You wanted to get rid of me?"

"Sure. I was worried sick, after Warren found your ad in the personals. He wanted to see you, and I tried to argue him out of it."

"Why?"

She made a pleading, palms-up gesture. "When you live as we do, cut off from our families, from our whole past lives, devoting ourselves to a cause which is legally treason—sedition —any contact with the world we've left is out of the question. It could imperil what we're trying to do. Roy agreed with me when I told him about it—he felt it was a terrible risk for Warren to take, to meet you."

"So you attempted to cut me off at the pass, before I could talk to him."

"I knew from what he'd told me that you were really a good friend. You wouldn't want anything to happen to him. So I thought if you were warned you were being tailed by someone who sounded like an F.B.I. man, you'd drop the idea of meeting him for fear you'd get him arrested. I hoped you'd just go home."

"Sorry I didn't, as it's turned out."

"I was more right than I thought." Her eyes rested vengefully on his bandaged shoulder. "Though I didn't expect anything like *this.* " Warren looked as though he might be asleep.

"Why the disguise when you talked to me?"

She grimaced. "Defense in depth. I couldn't *count* on your leaving town. So after I talked to you in the painting gallery, I went home and told Warren what I'd done. Different version. I explained to him how I had set up a meeting so that I could watch and find out whether anyone was following you. As a safety precaution. And I described to him the same fuzz type I had to you. Only I said I got the hell out of there as soon as I was sure you were being followed.

"I hoped that would scare him out of making contact with you. Naturally it didn't, and naturally he suspected I'd fabricated the whole incident—and why I had. So when he talked to you, he heard about my corroborating witness—the dark girl with the kerchief on her head."

"You tried," Warren said softly.

"Only—he figured it out," she said to me.

"I know how her mind works. Devious. Very devious."

She took his hand. "I didn't want to lose you!" Her voice was an anguished whisper. Here was the truth, beneath all her talk about the cause; giving me the picture of a girl in love who felt threatened by the opposing forces in her lover's life—his family and the past he has forsaken. Eve had wanted no risk to the status quo.

Warren seemed to drift off into sleep. The way Eve hovered over him made three a crowd, so I returned to the kitchen.

How long, I wondered, before Roy would be back?

Gary sat at the table, with the light above it—a bulb hanging at the end of a cord, with a greasy parchment shade around it

—reading a paperback. Mick lay almost on his spine in a decaying chair by the door. I took a rocker in one corner. I hadn't seen the rest of the house, but this room seemed to be living room as well as kitchen.

Mick reached over and flicked on a radio that sat on a shelf by the window, but Gary looked up at once from his book and signed for him to turn it off. "He needs to sleep." He nodded in the direction of Warren's room. Hastily Mick shut it off.

"Oh, yeh. Didn't even think—"

A Kurt Vonnegut paperback lay next to a bottle of detergent above the sink. I picked it up and started reading—something to pass the time.

Roy was gone a long while. It was more than twelve hours now since Warren had been shot . . . I wondered how far they'd driven to find a drugstore. Wouldn't want to burglarize one too near, that was sure.

At last we saw lights arc through the yard and heard the sound of the panel truck pulling up next to the house. A minute later Lucia and Roy came in.

Eve appeared in the door from the storeroom.

"Here." Roy extended his hands. Obviously pleased with himself, he held out two wholesale-size pharmaceutical jars— one a quarter full of pink capsules, the other containing white tablets. "Tetracycline. And codeine."

Eve took them, with a radiant smile, and went off to dose up Warren.

Lucia stepped to the kitchen table and emptied onto it the contents of a paper bag. Canadian dollars cascaded onto the white enamel.

"A city drugstore, as you can see," Roy pointed out. "Little country store wouldn't do that much business in a week." He threw a glance over at me. "For the cause, Little Lord Fauntleroy; it needs financing."

*   *   *

70

Soon after, they put me to bed. Roy handed me a rolled-up sleeping bag he'd brought from one of the front rooms of the house, and he and Gary, the latter with a flashlight, escorted me outside.

At the back of the house, in an angle between the outside wall of the kitchen and that of the storeroom, was an old-fashioned double-doored cellar entrance, set at an angle against the foundation. Roy threw back the doors and motioned me in first. I went down the steep concrete stairs, bending so as not to hit my head. The others followed, and Roy pulled the chain on a light hanging from the ceiling near the steps.

This must be the workroom I'd heard mentioned. A small room completely floored with concrete, containing some kind of printing equipment, a long table, a kitchen chair, and a canvas army cot. A pair of fluorescent tubes in a battered fixture had been installed in the center of the ceiling; unlit at present.

"You can bed down there." Roy nodded toward the cot in one corner. He turned, ready to leave. "And don't waste your time trying to bust the cellar door open. The noise would only disturb your good friend, and you wouldn't get out anyway."

Gary had already ascended the steps, and Roy followed. Halfway up, he stopped, leaned back into the cellar and said, "We'll let you out first thing in the morning."

The doors thumped closed and I could hear the rasp of metal on metal as they were fastened in some way. Silence then, but after a few more minutes—as I stood partway up the steps inspecting the doors above me—I heard voices again, just outside. Then there was a hollow clang as something was thrown on top of the cellar entrance; a moment later came a thud, and another and another, as a collection of objects was heaped on the doors to weight them down.

I turned away. There were no windows. A plank door hung in the center of the wall to my left. I opened it, with not much in the way of expectations. On the other side was a smaller

71

room with only an earth floor—and no windows. My only reaction to it was that this would be a good place to bury a body you wanted to get rid of.

After glancing around at the printing operation, I spent a few minutes reading the beginning of a pamphlet I picked out of the top of a box. A diatribe against democratic government—a mosaic of quotes from the whole hierarchy of modern revolutionists . . . Unite in the name of brotherhood, unite against the oppressors and pull them down, destroy them on behalf of the exploited millions . . .

I unrolled the sleeping bag on top of the cot.

I was exhausted after the long, traumatic day, but I was sure I couldn't sleep. I lay down, with the light still on, and studied the floor beams above me.

My longevity, I could guess, was directly connected with Warren's state of health. Warren would let no harm come to me, and eventually he would work out some agreement with the others to let me go—care being taken, certainly, that I not find out where this refuge of theirs was located.

Without Warren . . . but then why should I worry about any such contingency?—the bullet was out, and we had tetracycline for him.

I wondered what Julie was doing. Probably wasn't speaking to me any more. Though if anything as obscure as a shooting in a place like the Hôtel Genève made headlines, maybe she'd figure out what had happened . . .

I opened my eyes and fuzzily realized that I'd fallen asleep with the light on. I got up from the cot and staggered, on legs as heavy as lead, the few feet to where I could pull the string that hung from the naked bulb.

As I felt my way back to my bed in the darkness, remembering not to stumble over the cartons of pamphlets I remembered were somewhere on the floor, I tried to think of some reason —any reason—why Warren's little group would let me go. None occurred to me.

72

6

Mick and Gary let me out at about eight in the morning. Mick had a rifle in his hands, which he kept pointed vaguely in my direction as we rounded the corner of the house and went up the rickety steps to the side porch. I looked questioningly at it.

"Roy said I was to make sure you didn't leave us."

I noticed then that the panel truck was nowhere in evidence in the yard, and assumed Lissing had gone off somewhere.

I went at once in to see Warren.

It was evident that he was not doing too well.

"I suppose it's inevitable that he'd have a lot of inflammation there," Eve said. And I began to worry again about the quality of my surgery.

Best not to disturb the bandages, we decided. We'd give the wound a chance to heal, relying on the tetracycline to ward off any incipient infection.

"I only wish Roy'd thought to bring a thermometer—" Eve said, her hand on Warren's pasty forehead. "As long as he was in a drugstore anyway—"

"Where is Roy, anyhow?"

"He went to meet somebody."

"Don't ask questions, Lex—" Warren said.

After I'd had my breakfast and had shaved with the community electric razor that was kept in the bathroom, they shut me up again in the cellar. This time with Gary for company, because he was working down there, printing a new page of their latest pamphlet.

"Wanna help?" he asked.

"Afraid not."

He shrugged. "Makes no difference to me. I just thought you might like something to do to pass the time."

"Why am I shut in today when yesterday you let me run loose?"

"Yesterday was different—we couldn't do our regular work on account of Warren, so it was just as easy to keep a watch on you. Besides, no one wanted to upset Warren by putting you in chains or anything like that—he had it bad enough as it was."

"But today's different—"

"Warren knows the same as the rest of us that we can't have you splitting and bringing the pigs back here with you. Don't think that just because he and you used to be friends he's any different from the rest of us. What we're working for is more important to him than any other thing. Same as all of us."

"And you really want the violent overthrow of the government, like—"

"There's no other way. Man, people by the millions are being had and you sit there and condone it. Or applaud, maybe?"

We didn't exactly argue; he told me how it was. The whole world mess and what it needed to set it to rights.

I watched him as he ran the offset printing machine—a young man with the flame of idealism burning bright within him. Though many of his tenets scarcely differed from my own, where we diverged was on the means of achieving the greatest good for the largest number.

"How do you support this outfit here?" I asked him. "Got a grant from Chairman Mao?"

74

"Oh, we got jobs. Roy works at a garage—that's where he was yesterday when Eve called; we don't have a phone here. Mick's got a job at a hamburger place."

"How about you?"

"I'm between jobs. I was working as a dishwasher at one of the resorts, but got laid off. Lately I've been helping Lucia in the garden."

"What do you do with the sheep? Or are they yours?"

"They're camouflage, partly. Make it look like a real farm. But we're going to sell the lambs—"

At a little after ten Mick came to the cellar entrance and handed down sandwiches and a container of milk with two glasses. Gary made me stand back, on the far side of the cellar, while the door was open.

"How's Warren?" Gary asked.

"Running a fever, for sure." I could see Mick's face as he leaned down into the cellar opening. He looked worried. "I suppose that's natural, though, with what he's been through."

"Well, *some* fever; not too much, I hope." Gary squinted up at him.

"Wait and see, I guess. Listen, I got to get going, or I'll be late."

Neither of them was paying any attention to me. I could have made it up the stairs and away before the door was shut and locked on us again. But I didn't feel like taking off—not till I knew Warren was going to be all right.

So Gary and I spent the afternoon in the cellar.

"Mick went off to fry hamburgers?"

"Yeh."

"How does he get to his place of employment?" I'd been under the impression we were a long way, here, from anything but nature.

"Bicycle," said Gary. "Since the truck isn't here."

I wondered where he kept the bicycle.

By three Gary was tired of his printing chores. He pounded

on the floorboards above us, and after a minute or so Lucia came to the cellar doors and called in through a crack.

"Roy's not back yet. You can't come up."

"Oh, shit!"

"That's what he said—not to let Lex up unless he or Mick is here."

So we waited.

Late in the afternoon we heard the sound of the truck outside, and a few minutes later Roy let us out. He had the rifle with him—which he kept pointed quite definitely at me.

Lucia was fixing dinner. As I passed her, I saw from her indrawn lips, and by the way she stirred the soup in a pot on the stove, in jerks, that she was extremely upset.

"I don't see why not," she said to Roy—apparently continuing an argument interrupted moments before.

"No. Positively no! No doctor!"

Gary and I went straight in to see Warren.

My heart sake when I caught sight of him. His face was flushed, his eyes bright with fever, the skin stretched tight over the bones of his face.

"I've doubled his tetracycline," Eve volunteered. She looked haggard. "I thought it wouldn't do him any harm."

"Good idea," Gary said.

"Hi, Lex." Warren summoned a smile.

"How you feel?" I asked him.

"A little lightheaded."

"How's your shoulder?"

"Hurts like hell. What would you expect?" He turned his eyes to Gary. "It ought to start improving by tomorrow—don't you think?"

"You're asking a dropout that never even made vet school?" But there was rather a sickly look on Gary's face.

"Evie," said Warren, "you go out and get some air or something. You've been in this room all day. All night, too, for that matter. I'm a convalescent now—"

She was reluctant to leave him. "I won't be gone long." She laid her hand for a moment on his arm, and then went out.

"You, too, Gary—you've been a shut-in all day in the cellar. Why don't you go pick peaches or something?"

The fat boy seemed undecided. He looked first at Warren, then at me, then into the kitchen. He shrugged. "See you later."

As he went back through the kitchen and out the door, I saw that Roy, from his seat in the tumble-down chair by the door, had a clear view of me in the chair beside the bed—the place where Eve had sat and which I'd dropped into as she went out. Roy would keep an eye on me.

"Lex—" Warren spoke in almost a whisper. "We'd better figure a way to get you out of here. But first there's something I want you to know about. It's what I came to tell you yesterday morning, then—well, I've been on the horns of a dilemma about it. To tell you is a betrayal of my group. But I don't agree with them about this thing they propose to do—I think it would be a tragedy of the first water. They—" There was movement behind me, and he broke off.

Lucia had come from the kitchen. "Special for you, Warren. You need a light diet, with your fever." She set down a steaming bowl on the upended box serving as bedside table, at Warren's elbow.

"Chicken soup?" He sat up, grimacing with pain as he did so, and braced himself against a pair of pillows. "Lucia's never heard of canned soup," he told me. "This is the real thing."

Her effort to fight down the little smile of pride did not quite succeed. There was an extra dimension, no doubt—a sense of mission—to the care and feeding of revolutionaries, which made even of kitchen chores a sacred rite.

Lucia sat with us while Warren ate. She was Mick's girl, I had gathered, but I could see that she loved Warren also, as though he were her brother; they were all close, in this group —relying on one another, united against the enemy who were everywhere around them.

77

By the time Warren had finished his soup, Eve was back, and there was no further chance for me to learn what it was that Warren had wanted to tell me.

The rest of us had dinner in the kitchen. The others asked Roy guarded questions about the success of his day, and he gave veiled answers. I could gather only that he had driven somewhere in order to see and talk with another member of their group—someone named Ronald, who had made a trip from elsewhere especially to confer with Roy. Ronald had said he would be ready when the time came.

Ready for what? I wondered.

Roy turned to me. "You read our pamphlet?"

"Yes, as it happens—nothing else to do while Gary was printing away down there."

"What did you think of it?"

"Pretty purple, elementary stuff."

Roy nodded. "It's not for the college set. But you'd be surprised how many people there are that a pamphlet like this appeals to. People who've had nothing all their lives, their parents and grandparents had nothing all their lives . . . They get a glimpse of an alternative to being ground down, and it's like a religious conversion."

The resentful fire I'd long ago come to know as part of Roy burned in his eyes. "You're one of the few, aren't you? The very few at the top of the heap who divide up amongst themselves—"

"My family's well off. Though not in a class with your buddy Warren's. And I believe—the same as you do—that people should not go hungry, that the color of a man's skin shouldn't keep him from having—"

No one convinced anyone else of anything. Naturally. We even agreed that power corrupts—usually. I asked him who would have the power after his revolution, and wouldn't it corrupt whoever had it? In answer, Roy delivered an essay on the marvels wrought in the People's Republic of China. I

78

thought of all those bodies that had floated downstream from inner China, bobbing putrescent in the estuaries, clogging the rice paddies, during the Cultural Revolution, and I saw myself and most of my acquaintances drifting out to sea off Manhattan with the sewage.

Warren had fallen asleep after eating his soup, and so Eve joined us for dinner. By the time we finished, Mick had come back. Roy left us—a delightful development to me anytime— and disappeared into the front of the house. The rest of us sat around with our coffee.

I studied Eve, across from me, with her face that was somehow both childish and voluptuous. I wondered what had oriented her toward revolution. A bent of her own? Or had she gotten mixed up in it because of Warren?

"What were you going to do with your artistic ability?" I asked her. "Before you got locked into this movement?"

"I never got far enough to decide. The other was more important. Taking the time to paint or draw seems selfish when there's so much else that needs doing."

I disagreed. "But art's *very* important—" I began.

"Eve is our expert shoplifter," contributed Mick. "None of us'd have threads if she didn't bring 'em to us."

I don't know why I was shocked. Eve's was a case of dedication again, like Lucia's to the kitchen. Nothing dishonest about a little thievery from Eve's point of view—it was a necessity, for the cause. The personal risk was part of her contribution.

She was also attacking the System, wasn't she? Part of her credo—

Warren was still asleep when I went off to my prison to bed. He looked a poor color, though I hoped that was only the light in the storeroom; Eve had brought a table lamp from somewhere else in the house and placed it on the floor behind a box, to serve as a sickroom light. She was hovering over him, leaning down and watching him breathe, when I looked in for a minute.

What was it he had wanted to tell me? Something important

79

enough that he had changed his mind, the night before last, about not seeing me again. Maybe tomorrow—

I knew now what it was they had put on top of the doors to the cellar to insure my staying down there. It was a large galvanized tub, and it had been filled with firewood from a stack by the kitchen porch. The tub and the split logs waited by the doors for use again tonight.

I went reluctantly down the stairs.

There was no doubt in my mind the next day that something must be done for Warren. No matter what his friends wanted or didn't want to do, they were going to have to get him to a hospital—and fast.

I looked at his waxy face with the sweat standing on it, his body that seemed, in this short time, to have wasted away. He was shivering.

"Not doing so good, I think," he volunteered.

"Have you taken the bandages off to look at it?" I asked Eve.

She shook her head. "I was afraid of infection getting in. You think—"

"I think the infection's in already."

I went back to the kitchen and washed my hands thoroughly at the sink, relaying to Gary, my paramedical cohort, the fact that the patient looked to me to be very bad indeed. He followed me into the sickroom.

Warren's skin was burning to the touch. I pulled off the tape and lifted the bandage, readying myself for what might be under it. Even so, I was hardly prepared, and I think I flinched, with an involuntary impulse that passed away in a shudder. The wound was suppurating—a term I'd read for years and now I saw what it meant. The little Band-Aids I'd hoped would hold the edges of skin together were soaked through and I pulled them off.

"Pretty bad, I expect. Isn't it." Warren stated flatly.

"Yes, it's pretty bad." I was looking at the red angry edges of the wound—puffed and discolored. "You'd know that anyway, from the chills and fever."

Eve looked around at me, her face quite drained of color. "We'll have to get him a doctor, whether Roy wants to or not."

As she spoke, Roy's tall, lank form appeared in the doorway. "What are we going to do, whether I want or not?"

"Get a doctor." She gestured at the bed, where Warren was racked with harder chills than ever; I tucked the heavy brown blanket more closely about him.

Roy stalked forward to look. He leaned over, touched Warren's hot skin and shook his head at the ghastly, gaping mess that was his shoulder. Even the sneering, flinty Roy was taken aback, I could see. He grasped Warren by the other shoulder —the good one—and pressed it. "We'll take you to a hospital. No other way."

Warren closed his eyes and barely nodded his head. "Maybe I can get by without their finding out who I am. As 'Haywood'—" And I remembered the printed card stuck in the bellpush slot at his apartment. He had established a whole new identity here in Canada. Whether it would stand up under scrutiny, of course—

Eve—seeming almost giddy with relief—was already preparing the patient for departure. I helped, clumsily putting fresh gauze and adhesive over our cause for alarm.

"Where will you take him?" asked Gary as Mick stooped down and lifted Warren in his arms to carry him out.

"Montreal. I don't know anything about the hospitals up in this part of the country. Mustn't be too close to home, either, for security reasons."

Sure. Security first—always.

Eve shook into her cupped palm a quantity of the codeine tablets and the pink antibiotic capsules; poured them into an empty aspirin bottle that lay by Warren's drinking glass. She went into the kitchen. "Where's Mick's thermos?" I heard her ask Lucia as I passed through on my way out the door.

Roy and Mick were settling Warren in the back of the panel truck, with pillows, and with blankets under and on top of him —though nothing now could stop his shivering. It did not help that the day was raw and damp—the warm weather having vanished overnight. Rain clouds hung low over the hills.

"I'll ride with him," I said; with not a clue as to whether they would let me.

Roy turned his pale eyes on me with as much dislike as ever. "As a matter of fact, that's correct. You *will* ride with him. Turns out we're lucky to have brought you with us. You can deliver Warren to the emergency room after I drop you off. Give me a chance to get safely away."

Eve hurried to the open back doors of the truck and started to climb in.

"No." Roy grabbed her by the arm.

If she hadn't had both hands full—a thermos in one, the pills in the other—she would have clawed him.

"I'm going!" she said, her voice loaded with venom. "You can't *keep* me from going!"

"Eve, we can't afford to lose you. I'm taking a risk as it is, but we'll keep the risk to the minimum—me and the truck. If the fuzz nab us, you'll be needed here more than ever. It's just lucky we have Lex to see Warren safely into the hands of the doctors. You trust Lex, don't you? I mean about this—he's Warren's oldest friend."

He signaled Mick. "Hold onto her till we're gone—it's for her own good; for all of us." He gave a grim smile. "I'm sorry, Eve. No other way."

Mick had her, holding onto her arm, and Lucia stepped up on the other side to put an arm comfortingly around her shoulders. Tears streamed down Eve's cheeks. "But I'll never see him again! You can't do this! Whether he lives or dies, I'll never see him—" She choked to a stop.

"We've got to get going." Roy turned away and got into the front of the truck.

82

"Lex!" Eve held out to me the thermos and the little bottle of pills. "He'll need these in another twenty minutes. Please—"

I took them, though I doubted the medication would make any difference—it hadn't done much good so far. And impulsively I kissed her on the cheek. "I'll take the best care of him I can—"

I got in, the doors were closed on us by Gary, and we were away.

"How's it going?" I asked as we bumped down the farm lane toward the road.

"Not good." Even in the dimness of the truck body I could make out the queer, desperate look on his face. "Lex—Lex, I'm scared green."

I reached over and laid my hand on his wrist, under the heavy blanket, and pressed it—reassuringly, I hoped. Even covered up by the blanket, he seemed so frail. "Hang on, Badger. We won't be too long now." I hoped not, anyway.

"Want some water? I guess that's what's in the thermos—" It was all I could think of to do for him.

"Yeh. Thanks."

I unscrewed the top and half-filled it. Held his head so he could drink. His hair was sodden with perspiration.

We had turned onto the road now, and it was a relief to be at last away from the farm. An even greater relief to know we were en route to a hospital. In an hour and a half—about—we'd be there.

I peered at my watch in the gloom. Seven-twenty-five. Must remember to give him his medication in twenty minutes.

Apropos of nothing, it occurred to me that today must be Monday. The time at the farm had been a kind of limbo, where days of the week had no meaning.

It began to rain—softly at first, and then turning into a downpour. Damn! I thought. The weather would slow us up.

As the rain drummed on the metal roof over our heads,

Warren stirred, taking one hand from under his cover. He beckoned me to lean close so that he could say something.

"What I wanted to tell you before . . . and hadn't the chance—"

I nodded.

He turned his head slightly—gauging the distance between us and Roy Lissing in the driver's seat—lifting his eyes to the roof. He seemed reassured—Roy couldn't hear us over the noise.

"I've parted company, in some respects, with the rest of them. I'm convinced that revolution of the kind we've worked for will never be achieved in the States. We lost our chance in sixty-eight; seventy. The others don't think so—they still expect to bring it off."

He closed his eyes and hunched himself into a tighter ball for warmth, as a new attack of chills racked his body.

I waited.

His eyes opened. "What I wanted to tell you: they're going to kill Praeger."

I looked at him, startled, not sure I'd heard correctly. "Kill Hugo Praeger?"

"That's it."

"But *Praeger*—so much of what he's fought against is what your group has attacked also. Most of the things he wants to do politically even Roy can't disapprove of!"

"That's right. They agree about the gains we'd make under him. But not enough. Not enough." He was finding it hard to speak; perhaps because of the shivering. "They feel that the 'compromise benefits'—as they call them—that Hugo Praeger would . . . give the people . . . would scotch all hopes of a genuine revolution."

"Oh."

"I'm for Praeger, myself. He's great . . . Great . . ." He closed his eyes and it was a moment or two before he went on. "Should have had a man like that at the helm long ago." His teeth were

84

chattering now. "Things would've been different . . . Different."

He lapsed into silence and I sat there contemplating what he had told me.

To kill Hugo Praeger . . . The best hope the United States had had in many years . . . And to kill him *because* he was a man who believed in many of the things his assassins preached—

Warren struggled to sit up, and I adjusted his pillows so that his head was higher. "What was I saying?" he asked, his forehead puckered in an effort to remember.

"About Praeger."

"Yes. Praeger. He wants the things *I* want, you know." Reaching a hand from under his covers, he took my arm. "Praeger would give us a tremendous leap forward, Lex, in the way we should go. He would!" He seemed almost to be proselytizing.

"I quite agree. I told you that the other day."

"That's right, you did." He let go of me to pass his hand over his forehead, over his eyes. "What was it I wanted to say? . . . Oh, yes. I've tried to convince the others. My group. Convince them that Praeger being elected would be all to the good—we could go on from there, with further advances when we get the chance . . . Roy says no . . . Ronald says no. No half-measures. They want total revolution. All or nothing at all. So we mustn't have Praeger in office."

"They want a *conservative* to be elected?"

"Yes. Conservative. Reactionary. The more reactionary the better, so there's provocation—something really to revolt against."

"That's insane!"

"Yes. And all because we lost our chance." He shook his head, closed his eyes. After a minute or two while he tried to control the chattering of his teeth, he went on. "There aren't enough people who advocate the violent overthrow of the United States Government. Not enough to bring it off. There *are* groups, working separately all over the country, but they

85

have no unified leadership. We've been hoping to get them all together. We never will . . . I know that now. It's the impossible dream."

He huddled against his pillow, wrapping himself more closely in his blanket. Near to tears, I looked down at him. A boy with a tender heart, a love of the underdog; an idealist. I could not see him taking part in any bloody revolution. Nor could he now, I realized. When he'd joined the ranks of dissidents, what he'd been opposing was the bloody Vietnam War. There had been no bloodless alternatives between which he could choose.

We had turned onto another road and picked up speed.

"Lex—" Warren said beside me, and I noticed suddenly that the rain had let up. I started to caution him that Roy might hear, but it was already too late.

"You've got to warn Praeger what he's up against," he said. I cocked an ear and decided that the squeak and slap of the windshield wipers probably interfered sufficiently with sound from the truck's rear.

I leaned near Warren again. "When will they? How?"

"Not till they're sure he'll be a candidate. How? Gun . . . However it can be managed."

"You okay back there?" Roy called.

"He's got hard chills. Don't spare the horses—" I frowned, trying to pin down what it was that had been bothering me a couple of minutes before; something plucking away at the back of my mind; something wrong.

"I'll get him there as fast as I can. Listen, Lex—when you turn Warren in at the hospital, remember his name's Bill Haywood. That's all you know. You're a passer-by who found him collapsed in a doorway. A friendly guy in a truck gave you a lift to the hospital and you don't know my name."

"Anything you say."

But now that I had time to think, I wondered—for the first time since we'd left the farm—why he felt he could trust me.

In his book I was one of the villains. I had come to Canada specifically to take Warren away from the movement and restore him to the Establishment in the United States. And now was my chance, as he must see it—wasn't it?

"Of course," he was saying, "you never saw the farm or any of us—no matter who you talk to now or later."

"Yeh. I know."

The conversation (if that's what you could call it) died.

I checked my watch.

"Time for your pills and such," I said. "Four pink ones?" He made no sign and I thought maybe he was asleep. But he opened his eyes when I propped up his head, and swallowed the capsules with some water.

"How about the codeine?"

"Yes." His long lashes rested for a moment on his sallow cheeks. "Two. No—no, three."

I thought two was the dose, but I gave him three.

His eyes seemed to have sunk even deeper into their sockets. It was as though he looked out at me from another world—and that thought gave me the shivers.

"Tell Julie I've thought of her so often, these years." I think what he was doing was smiling, but the effect was ghastly. "She thinks I never appreciated her. I did. Just . . . too much of . . . a bastard to have told her so."

He stopped, panting.

"Thank her for the watch?"

"Yeh, I'll do that," I said.

I wished that he wouldn't sound so much as if he were making his last will and testament.

"Say everything to my mother that needs saying—"

"Sure."

He slept then.

I sat there next to him, my spirits leaden. No thoughts, even, passed through my head, only a montage of long-ago scenes. Warren at the tiller of his first sailboat; Warren sitting white-faced, clutching his ankle the time he'd sprained it jumping from our garage roof; squatting across from me at our campfire, face grotesquely marked with burnt cork to simulate Indian war paint, in the days when he had been Wise Badger and I had been Running Coyote; gleeful and intent as he propped a water-bomb atop a door for the benefit of Mr. Beiner, our most disliked teacher in fifth grade; bemused, entranced, the summer he had become serious about a girl for the first time—Jenny, her name had been, and he hadn't known she slept with every boy she met . . . Warren at Exeter; a freshman at Harvard, before we'd begun so definitely to drift apart; Warren at Julie's debut party . . . And I wondered what she'd be doing now . . . *Tell Julie I've thought of her so often, these years*—

I'd come full circle, back to Warren lying shivering in his blankets with a putrid hole in him.

I wished that I had some confidence he was going to survive.

I thought of Julie now. Funny that she'd been in my mind so much of the time since I'd seen her in Montreal.

Come to think of it, I'd spent years, hadn't I, trying not to think of Julie at all; just as I'd expended every effort, when she was around, to hide from those present my utter vulnerability where she was concerned. Not being a masochist, I'd have been mad ever to let her find out the effect she had on me.

And I'd hoped my condition was something I'd outgrow. I should have; because the truth, as I'd told myself often enough, was that I didn't even like her. It was just that the slightest flutter of her eyelashes . . .

Warren was still sleeping, but he seemed disturbed. He was muttering something unintelligible and moving the fingers of his left hand restlessly along the edge of his cover.

I checked my watch. Fifty minutes since we'd left the farm. Another forty yet to go . . . If Roy hadn't lied about his intentions.

Ah. That. At last I allowed myself to face the doubts I'd been trying not to recognize.

Had I ever believed, even back at the farm, that Roy Lissing would let us both go? He couldn't trust me—that was for sure; and I knew too much about their organization. I could probably —in spite of the precautions taken—find the farm again, with help from the police.

And Warren? Could he trust Warren, after the schism in their leadership occasioned by the plan to assassinate Hugo Praeger? Mightn't he even welcome the opportunity to rid their group of its now-dissident member, one who argued for moderation when moderation was the last thing Lissing wanted?

I got up on my knees; looked out to see if I could tell anything about where we were. Still countryside—rolling hills, lots of trees. No more rain, the road was dry.

The terrified high-pitched cry beside me almost raised the hair on my scalp. It was so sudden, so unexpected. So primal.

Roy hit the brake. "Hey, what—"

Warren was sitting up, looking frantically around him. "Eve? *Eve!*"

I took hold of him by both arms. "Warren! You're okay, Warren."

"What's the matter with him?" Roy called.

Warren was staring straight toward me but beyond, as if I weren't there. "Eve, where are you?"

"He wants Eve," I told Roy.

There was a short silence. Then, "You mean he's delirious."

I didn't bother to answer him. "Warren, you're okay. Lie down. I'm here. I'll be with you all the time. Lie down."

I hunted around for something to use for a compress. Nothing. No handkerchief, no Kleenex. I pulled out the tail of my by-now very mussed shirt and tore off a piece; not easy, the shirt was still new. I unscrewed the cap from the thermos and wet the piece of cloth. Forced Warren back and laid the compress on his burning forehead. He fought me. "Got to go . . . We can't . . . can't stay here . . . can't stay—"

The compress heated through so fast . . . I'd take it off, unfold it, and wave it through the air to cool it; pour a little more water on and reapply it.

He would lapse into silence for a few minutes and then suddenly cry out again. Sometimes I could understand him, sometimes not. Once he mentioned Ronald, quite loudly and distinctly, and I knew Roy must have heard.

What was it, I started wondering again, that had bothered me, way back early in the ride? Something about the truck, or the trip itself—the trip to Montreal.

Never mind, though, what I'd thought awhile ago. What mattered was our situation as I saw it now . . .

If there had been a time—back at the farm, though even then it was unlikely—when Roy would have accepted the risk of letting Warren go, that time was now irrevocably gone. Lissing could never relinquish to anyone a cohort babbling deliriously of anything that came into his head . . . Because next, of course, he could be talking of Praeger—

The truck slowed, and I leaned to the side as we turned sharply to the right.

It was then I knew what had bothered me earlier, because the turn brought back the recollection of that other moment, when we had come to a full stop and then had gone to the left.

Suddenly I knew—clear as day. We were not on our way to Montreal.

I had tried, on the way out of the city, to keep track of our route. So the pattern of turns and the time between changes of direction had stayed in my mind. Leaving the farm, we should have gone left. We had. After about ten minutes we should have turned right. Instead we had gone to the left. Warren had been telling me at that point of the plan to kill Praeger, and so the significance of Roy's change from our expected route had not come through to me till now.

And where were we? Not on the good highway I remembered —the one which would have put us in the environs of Montreal. This road wasn't even paved—I could hear the barrage of little

90

stones thrown up by the tires against the underpart of the truck.

We were starting uphill.

I got to my knees, far enough back so that Roy wouldn't feel me breathing down his neck, and looked out over the seats in front, through the windshield, and as well as I could, through the windows to either side. We were going up the steep incline of a dirt road, and there was solid forest all around us.

"Lex—some water?"

My relief was enormous, as I looked to the side and saw Warren with his eyes focused on me.

In my haste to pour him some water, I almost knocked over the thermos.

I held the cup for him to drink. "You've been out of your head," I said softly.

"Not surprised." He finished drinking, glanced around at the inside of the truck. "Where are we?"

"What's he doing—raving again?" Roy asked.

"He's okay now, he's conscious. I've been soaking his head with cold water."

"Oh, good! That's great. Hang in there, Warren—"

I leaned down so that I could whisper in Warren's ear. "Listen—he's not taking us to Montreal. We're deep in the Laurentians. Mountain road. Feel us going up?"

He nodded.

He struggled to a sitting position. The look of him shocked me to the core. He was like a caricature of my old friend—hair sodden and unkempt, mustache too big for his shrunken face, two days' growth of beard shadowing his cheeks and chin, eyes wide and staring. The classic image of a wild-eyed revolutionary.

"You've got to get away," he breathed.

"Both of us."

Exhaustedly he shook his head. "No. Not me."

"Yes. He's going to dump you in the wilderness. I'm sure of it." We were going up ever more steeply, and I trusted that the laboring of the engine in lower gear would make it hard for Roy to hear us. But I leaned closer. "Does he carry a gun?"

"Revolver. Under the seat," he said fuzzily.

"Are you with me if I can jump him?"

"I owe you that, Lex. We could turn him loose afterward."

I bent my head to the floor and looked under the seats in front of me. No gun. But of course he wouldn't have left it there, within my reach!

I got on my knees again. "No chance along here," I reported, mouthing the words. To our right the ground fell sharply away; if I tried now to grab Roy, we could all go over the edge. But there was my objective, four feet away, where Roy's scrawny neck supported his rather small head (made to seem a little larger, with the beard).

Warren touched my wrist. "I'm sorry, Lex. Sorry I got you into this."

"You didn't." I raised my voice for Roy. "Oughtn't we to be getting to the highway soon?"

"Not long," the answer came back. "I took a shortcut. Sorry about the rough ride."

But you don't take a shortcut in the wrong direction.

Warren was trying to whisper something. I leaned down to hear. "*Not* a shortcut. Shortcut would have been the toll road."

He looked up at me, shivering. "We may not come out of this. Either of us."

"I can't believe that, Badger." But I lied.

I waited for a chance to take on Roy Lissing.

I was crouched a little behind the driver's seat, ready to grab Lissing with an arm across his throat. I could see the road ahead, still angling up; could see that at the next turn we would head in toward the mountain slope, away from the drop. One of those hairpin turns, for which Roy would have to slow appreciably.

I had to pick someplace—might as well be here.

As we slowed and headed into the curve, I leaned forward. And it was then that I glanced out the left-hand window into the rear-view mirror; in it my eyes met the pale, feral eyes of the man at the wheel. He had swiveled the mirror to reflect the interior of the truck instead of the road behind him. As I would have done in his place.

I reached to clamp my forearm around his neck. He slammed on the brakes, and the truck slewed to one side, shuddering to a stop.

Before I could make my next move, he had twisted in my grasp. I found myself looking, at very close range, down the smooth black barrel of a revolver.

I let go of him. No choice.

The engine had stalled as we stopped. Roy opened the door and slid out. Keeping his eyes and the gun on me, he reached back in and plucked the keys from the ignition.

"Now come on out here," he directed me. I climbed over the back of the seat, set the emergency brake in passing, and got out, bumping my head on the doorframe.

He backed away, keeping the gun on me and a safe distance between us. One side of his mouth quirked up into a sort of snarl, framed unpleasantly in his beard.

"Okay, now walk," he said. "Over there." He gestured off toward a stand of pines on the slope beyond the road.

"Why?"

"Because I want you the hell off the road. This is as far as you're going with us."

We were clear out of civilization, here. Not a human habitation in sight anywhere, not even any farmland. There were only the pine trees all around us, and the narrow dirt road disappearing above us around the shoulder of the mountain a couple of hundred yards farther on. The way we had come was visible only to the last hairpin turn. This was probably ski country, but in summer there would hardly be much of a traffic jam on the roads. We hadn't passed another car since we'd started up the mountain.

I could hear scraping behind me, and the sound of something rubbing against the inside of the truck. Warren was trying to pull himself up and make it into the driver's seat.

I didn't want him in the line of fire and so I moved—in the direction Roy had indicated.

If I could get behind a tree . . . Or a rock . . . I scanned the ground before me—a stony slope with no cover till the stand of trees about sixty feet away. I tried to guess what Roy meant to do. He intended to kill me, that was certain. And he wanted me far enough from the road that I wouldn't be found—not easily or soon.

Halfway to the trees the ground fell away fairly sharply into a little saucerlike depression filled with scrub. Only three feet deep or so, but anything that fell into it would be well hidden. I must skirt well around it or he'd drop me there as I passed.

I walked slowly, looking behind me every step or two, and Roy came after, trailing near enough to keep me in excellent range.

Suddenly the truck horn began to sound.

"Cut that out!" Roy shouted, and I turned to see him looking back, the revolver, as he twisted his head, pointed not quite at me.

Yet he wasn't near enough for me to rush him.

Nor was there any shelter close by for which I could possibly make a dive. I had to head for the stand of pines—still quite a distance off.

I had never known I could run so fast. Or that it could take so nightmarishly long to cover that short a distance. He fired twice. The first shot went by me. I stumbled and almost fell; recovered. It was hard to keep my footing on the uneven ground, on a slope which went up to one side of me and down

94

on the other. The truck horn still sounded, one blast after another.

Almost within reach of the trees . . . I took a long leap to the right from the jagged top of one rock to the rounded surface of another. As I landed, I heard the thunk of a bullet into one of the tree trunks ahead of me, and the report of the gun behind.

I flung myself into the shelter of the trees.

I looked back. Roy was running after me. I ducked further back among the pine trunks. There was no undergrowth—only the carpet of pine needles underfoot. The grove of trees was like a large room with many pillars. A poor place to hide—I could only take refuge behind a pine trunk and try to keep it between Roy and me without his finding out which one I'd chosen.

If he came in among the trees and I could jump him—

I heard his approach to the grove. His foot slipped on a rock and there was a shower of little stones falling down the slope. Then he was moving between the trunks of the first trees.

He stopped. At least I thought he had stopped, because there was no sound nearby, only the calls of birds at a little distance and the trickle of water not far away. Then, from no more than fifteen feet to the other side of my tree trunk, he let out an exclamation. I didn't catch what it was, but could not have missed its content of baffled anger.

He was moving back the way he had come.

I looked cautiously out, expecting to find him checking each tree trunk for my hiding place. Instead I saw that he was already out of the grove, scrambling hurriedly over the slope toward the truck.

And I saw why.

Down from the bend of the road above us came a group of hikers—four or five of them, all with back packs.

I left the shelter of the trees; leaped and ran over the slope after Roy.

Desperation seemed to give him wings. He was too far ahead

95

of me. I hadn't covered even half the distance by the time he reached the truck. "Warren!" I called. I stopped clambering, to straighten up and cup my hands around my mouth. "Warren! Badger! Get out! Get out of the truck!" There was no answer. The horn was no longer blatting, though I didn't know when it had stopped.

I scrambled forward again, aware that Roy had gotten into the truck. He started it and the engine turned over at once— the luck of the unjust.

The hiking group had put on speed as they came down the road—two of them well in the fore, sprinting for the scene of action.

"Stop him!" I called, for they were nearer than I. Roy was backing and filling now. It took him three hitches to turn the vehicle around. As he shot forward after the last hitch, one of the hikers caught hold of the door handle. I saw him clearly, etched indelibly as a thing may be in a moment of trauma—a slight, kinky-haired boy, his long thin arms reaching far out to the side of the truck, the pack on his back like a giant hump. The boy hung on for only a moment and then was flung aside, sprawling on hands and knees in the dirt of the road as the truck, with Warren still inside, barreled away down the mountain.

Part Two

7

I wondered whether she would still be in Montreal.

I put in a call, from Emilion, where I'd been brought by the hikers.

"Lex? Oh, Lex, are you all right?" Something flopped over in my chest at the note of caring in her voice; but that, I knew, was for Warren.

"I'm okay, Julie. But Warren's not. He—he was shot. Hit in the shoulder."

"Warren? Warren was shot?"

"Yes. Happened the day I didn't come to get you."

"Lex—how bad?"

"Well—it's not good, Julie. Trouble is the wound's infected."

"He's seen a doctor?"

"No."

There was a short silence. "Oh. Yes, I suppose . . . Where are you?"

"Up near Mont Tremblant . . . But I've told you only half the problem. Roy Lissing took off with Warren, claiming he was taking him to a hospital. I don't believe Roy—I've got the police looking for them."

"The police . . . Yes, I guess that's the only thing you could do . . . Look. I'll join you. Where will you be?"

"At Emilion. Take route fifteen—that's the big toll road—to Sainte Agathe. From there, route one-seventeen, toward Saint Jovite. Go just past Emilion. At the edge of town you'll find the Sûreté du Québec—a new brick building . . ."

I'd had no qualms about going to the police. As long as my best friend had been running his own life, I'd had no right to interfere. But now there was no alternative: if he didn't reach a hospital soon, he would be dead of his infection. And there was nothing that led me to believe Roy would take him anywhere for medical treatment. Roy couldn't afford the risk.

The hikers had come with me to Emilion—not so much, I thought, to oblige me as because their leader wanted to make sure I was not after all an escaped felon.

There had been two young men, two girls, and a somewhat older man—the latter probably with a heart of gold, but humorless, officious. And I didn't care for the obvious suspicion with which he treated me. It had been Roy who fled, not only from me but from them; hadn't he noticed that? Well, he had, but he questioned me anyway, delaying my taking off in pursuit of the panel truck. I filled him in as briefly as I could on what had happened, and thanked the thin, wiry kid who had actually reached the truck and grabbed the door handle. He'd gotten a pair of bruised and bleeding palms and a skinned knee for his pains. "Sure sorry I didn't make it!" he said.

We started off then down the road to the bottom of the mountain, the solid, square-built man who was my inquisitor still talking, explaining how they had been alerted by the truck horn and the shots.

"Glad you came along. If you hadn't—" Now that the danger and my wild exertions were over, I could feel my hands shake.

We hiked down into the valley where the main highway ran, and started along it toward the nearest town. Not long after, we were able to hitch a ride in the back of a stake truck. Selby

Grimser—that was the name of the group's leader—watched me carefully through his yellow-tinted glasses. All the way to Emilion.

I had supposed that the wilds up here were dotted with posts of the Royal Mounted Police. But our destination proved to be the local branch of the Sûreté du Québec—the provincial police force, comparable to the state police in the United States.

There was a split-level entrance, in the glassed-in front of the building, with a half-flight of stairs going down, and another going up. We trekked up the latter—overseen all the way by an officer who looked down at us through a window located on a sort of balcony. There was a door at the top of the stairs, but it was closed. We all filed past it to stand in a group before the counter at the window. There were three or four chairs against the wall, but no one sat down.

Grimser explained—as though I were deaf and dumb—what had happened to me. Officer Dubreuil—tall, brown-haired, wearing a name plaque on his shirt—listened, then questioned me in heavily accented English. Carefully he wrote down my answers—description of the truck, license number (I'd memorized it the first time I'd seen it, as we loaded Warren in for the trip into the country), Roy's description, Warren's (complete with both his real name and his Canadian one), and the fact that he was in grave physical condition, in urgent need of hospitalization.

Dubreuil then gave his attention to the radio-phone which sat on the counter, relaying into it, in French, the information I had given him.

He turned again to Grimser and me. "The patrol cars are informed. Also Montreal headquarters, who are in charge of the whole area—" With lavish gestures of both hands, he indicated the surrounding territory.

For the gleaning of further details I was turned over to Corporal Meunier—solid, black-haired, with a small mustache and large, liquid brown eyes—who took me through the door

99

at the top of the stairs into the further recesses of the building.

Whether Selby Grimser was disappointed not to see me led away in handcuffs, I don't know. When I left him, he was dictating a statement about what had happened, so far as he had witnessed it. All five hikers gave statements, I learned later, before going on their way—presumably to continue their interrupted hike.

By this time one piece of information had come in, in response to what Officer Dubreuil had fed into the radio-phone. The vehicle with the license number I had memorized was registered in the name of William R. Haywood, at Warren's address in Montreal.

No help at all in locating it now.

I sat in a chair by the corporal's desk. As I worked back, in the account I gave him, to the origins of the Roy Lissing–Warren Thayer situation—rephrasing occasionally when the French-Canadian's grasp of English failed him—Meunier's interest quickly escalated.

"Sergeant Perreault must hear this," he said. "One moment, please, monsieur."

When I continued, Sergeant Perreault had joined us. Perreault, a tall, gaunt man, late thirties, with beetling brows and a luxurious mustache, was the officer in charge of the sûreté post.

The sergeant left us, midway of my recital, to step into Dubreuil's bailiwick at the front, but he was back in a few moments.

I told them everything, beginning with Roy's seizing of the judge's daughter, in New York State, and his escape from prison; the homicide charge against Warren, which I hastened to explain was the result of very circumstantial evidence; my trip to Montreal and its purpose; the shooting; my detention at the farm; the drive this morning in the truck, and its end. I left out only Warren's story about the planned conspiracy; that information was for the F.B.I.

100

Dubreuil came in, during my recital, with a sheet of paper for the sergeant, which he glanced over, muttering to himself in French, and laid aside. I wondered whether it had anything to do with Warren.

I suddenly remembered something else. "I have the bullet that was taken out of his shoulder." I drew the slug, in its wrapping of Kleenex, from my shirt pocket and handed it over.

Perreault spread the tissue open and peered in at its contents. "Good. This will go in to the laboratory in Montreal. At headquarters." He put it carefully in the center of the desk.

He exchanged a glance with Corporal Meunier. "We got in touch a few minutes ago with the R.C.M.P.—"

"Air-sea?" I said, at a loss—for that was what I thought he had said.

"Royal Canadian Mounted Police. R—C—M—P." Of course. The French pronunciation of the letter r—

He was scanning again the paper Dubreuil had brought him. "I have here their reply. It says that on ten August, nineteen seventy-three, the F.B.I. requested the assistance of the R.C.M.P. in apprehending both these men. Roy Lissing, Warren Thayer. The request still stands."

Yes—Warren had said they'd had to move on, more than once.

The sergeant fixed me with his beetling gaze. "You realize, Mr. Norden, that when you took Mr. Thayer out of your hotel and helped him escape in your car, you were aiding a fugitive wanted by the Canadian police?"

So now we were getting to the tricky part. I had wondered all the way here whether I would be locked up as Grimser so obviously hoped.

I frowned. "How would I have known that?" I looked from one officer to the other. "Warren had committed no crime against the Canadian Government. I wouldn't have supposed he was wanted by the police, any more than were the thousands of American draft evaders your country has welcomed

101

on this side of the border."

It was the sergeant who answered. Corporal Meunier, with his less fluent English, watched and listened. "The killing of a law-enforcement officer—with which your friend is charged—is hardly to be compared with evading military service."

"But he's only charged, it's not proven. I'll never believe he could have killed a man. And as I explained, Sergeant Perreault, the purpose of my trip to Canada was to persuade Mr. Thayer to give himself up and stand trial. I never *stopped* trying to convince him to do that."

"Yet you cannot deny that you helped him flee the Hôtel Genève as the police were approaching."

I shook my head. "Someone tried to kill him. I wanted to get him away before whoever it was succeeded."

There was a dry, questioning look on Perreault's face. "You think this person would have broken down the door of your hotel room, where you both had found safety?" He looked away. "Your only course should have been to use the telephone in your room to summon the police—and wait for them there."

I shrugged. "When all this happened, Warren Thayer had done nothing wrong. He was shot at, wounded. He didn't have a gun, any weapon. It did not seem to me to be a crime to do as he asked—to help him get home. Though I argued all the way that he should go to a hospital instead."

"The *police* would have taken him to a hospital," Perreault said dryly. "You know that."

How simple if one does everything by the book!

"You're right. Of course you're right." Obviously if I had done as the sergeant suggested, Warren would by this time have been safely convalescent. "But how—" I looked from one to the other of the police. "How does one persuade oneself to play Judas to an old friend?"

It had been only midmorning when I got to Emilion—though it seemed then as if a whole day had already gone by. I dredged

102

up for Corporal Meunier, who was in charge of the case, every scrap of information I possessed: detailed description of the farm; all I could remember of our drive there from Montreal; the trip from the farmhouse to the mountain where I'd parted company with Warren and Roy—turns, estimated distances, times; the fact that Roy was employed at a garage, Mick at a hamburger place; descriptions of all of Warren's group; the name Ronald, even—whoever it might belong to. All of it was fed into the radio-phone—a sophisticated piece of equipment like a computer, which sent things variously either to the patrol cars in the area, or to Montreal headquarters, or to the R.C.M.P.

Specialists were being sent out to us from headquarters to help in the search; even a helicopter, which was promised for some time in the afternoon.

In the meantime I was dispatched with Corporal Meunier, in a patrol car, to the mountain area which had been identified by Grimser and his group, so that I could show him the spot at which I'd last seen Roy Lissing.

We went over the ground there, and some lab men from Montreal who joined us took casts of the tire tracks of the panel truck, where Roy had had to back and fill to get the thing headed downhill again. And they searched without any luck for the two bullets I said had been fired.

It was when we got back to the sûreté post that they let me call Julie, in Montreal.

Past noon by then, and someone kindly brought me a couple of hotdogs and a Coke from a diner across the highway.

There was no report on Roy's truck. Nor any report of Warren's turning up, either in a hospital or anywhere else.

A man from the R.C.M.P. had arrived from Montreal. O'-Neill—a change from all the French-Canadians. I told him at once about the plot to kill Praeger; the Royal Mounted, I had learned, where the federal police, equivalent to the F.B.I.—to whom he could relay my warning.

103

The helicopter arrived, and I was allowed to go aboard it along with Corporal Meunier. They hoped I could spot the farm.

We searched—with no luck.

There were not many farms through here, Meunier explained to me; the soil was too poor. Around Saint Jovite—yes, there were farms. And we hunted there without finding our objective. Most of this area was ski country—also developed into summer resorts, particularly around the lakes. Everywhere there were cabins, cottages—many of them second homes of people who lived in Montreal.

What good it would do Warren for us to find the farm I didn't know; he wouldn't be there. The news I kept anxiously awaiting was that the police had found him at some country doctor's office, or bedded in a hospital under another name.

When we finally got some news, though, it wasn't that. What came in on the helicopter radio was about the farm. An officer who'd been questioning store owners and real estate agents in little towns scattered throughout the countryside had learned that a man named William R. Haywood had leased a farm the year before. The people who lived on it answered near enough to the descriptions I'd given.

It was the right place. When we reached it, there were already two of the brown and yellow patrol cars belonging to the sûreté parked in the rutted drive.

We came down in the field in front of the house.

"Personne," said the officer who greeted us at the side door. *"Ils sont tous partis!"*

So Roy had come back and evacuated the whole group . . . Well, he'd had to. He'd known I would go to the police—that it would be a matter of only a few hours before we'd come zeroing in on his hideout.

I went over the house, together with Meunier. The beds, in the front rooms I'd never been in, were stripped; no clothes in the closets or drawers. A lone sock lay where it had been dropped on the floor. A pot of noodles sat on the stove, and some cucumbers on the drainboard, but the kitchen radio was gone. There were no cartons in the storeroom; the bed in there was stripped. On the floor next to the lamp, side by side, were the two pharmaceutical bottles containing Warren's medications. No further need for them when the group had departed—

The printing equipment was gone. Naturally. It was easy enough to transport in the panel truck. I stood in the cellar, looking around at what had once been my quarters—at the table, the kitchen chair, the cot (the sleeping bag was gone), the bare light bulb dangling by the stairs, the fluorescents affixed to the ceiling over the printing area. Impossible to believe that I had ever been held a prisoner here; impossible to believe I had stayed in this house, watching Warren rotting away, dying.

The door to the unfloored piece of cellar was closed. The police had already been down here, I knew; we'd met one of them coming up the steps as we came down. Yet I eyed the gray plank door uneasily. With a quiver of dread passing over me like a fever chill, I stepped past Corporal Meunier and opened the door to the room beyond.

It was empty. And I saw with relief that the earth of the floor was undisturbed.

I stepped back. Had I really supposed Roy might bury him there?

Julie was waiting for us at Emilion. She must have been watching from a window of the sûreté building as the helicopter landed in a field behind it; because as Meunier and I walked around the corner and skirted a blue car parked there, she came out the door and down the steps.

She flung herself on my chest. "Lex! Lex!" she breathed into my shirt.

I held her tight, aware of her scent, of her body pressed against mine, the top of her head against my cheek. Aware, too, of Corporal Meunier's delighted, appreciative smile as he waited for me at the steps.

I held her tighter. "There's no news of Warren yet—I'm sure you know that—"

She seemed to stiffen for a moment, and then she pulled away. "Yes—you found the farm and he wasn't there. So now what?" Her voice seemed curiously dead; a complete change from the emotion of a few seconds ago. Julie Thayer was back in her icehouse.

Meunier still waited. I did not know, actually—after Perreault's remarks about my aiding a fugitive—whether or not I was under some form of detention. I thought we'd better go inside.

"I don't know, Julie. I just don't know." I took her arm and introduced Meunier to her. "Corporal Meunier's in charge of the case."

"If you would like to join us, Miss Thayer," he suggested, "while I make my report to the sergeant—"

We found Sergeant Perreault studying the wall map.

"They may have gone to ground somewhere nearby," he said. "Lissing would be much pressed to have gone back the considerable distance from the mountain to the farm"—he indicated the two locations with a long, bony finger—"and have packed up and gotten clear before the roadblocks went up . . . Unless perhaps he did not go back, but left the area immediately. The others could have departed from the farm in another vehicle. If they have one?" He turned expectantly to me.

"Only a bicycle, so far as I know. But they had no plans to vacate the place when we left there this morning—and since there's no telephone, Lissing couldn't have warned them to get out except by coming back in person."

"Yes. As you say." His eyes roved again over the map, and he pulled at one end of his mustache. "We will continue to search."

"Can't *we* look, too?" Julie asked him. "I can take my car—"

106

"That would be of little use. And you have no authority. Besides, if they are still nearby, they are well hidden—you would find nothing."

"And will you find them?" she asked a little sharply.

He smiled. "We will try, Miss Thayer. We will try."

He said to me, "Please remain available—you and Miss Thayer. You are not being held, or charged, Mr. Norden. Inquiries have been made about you. There was nothing—unfavorable. We checked with Mr. Oliver Thayer, in New York, and he bears out your account of why you came here—the fact that he sent you. His word, of course—" Perreault's shrug summed up the undeniable influence of great wealth and eminent position. "But it is most of all a matter of your—intention. You had indeed no way of knowing that Thayer was wanted by the authorities here.

"You are free to go. But to you too I will say, do not attempt yourself to make any search. Such a thing could be dangerous for all concerned."

So we waited. We went out to the reception area by the stairs, and sat where we could look through the glass in the front. Dubreuil had been replaced in the communications room by another officer—a sleek, gigolo-looking man. He would let us know of any news.

"How was he—" she asked me. "When you left him?"

"Not good. They told you that, didn't they?"

"Yes. Sergeant Perreault gave me a rundown on everything. But you were with him, so—"

"Well, he'd been delirious for a while, but came out of it a bit. He was clear in the head at the last—he got help for us. Crawled from the back of the truck into the front seat and started hitting the horn. That brought a bunch of hikers that were nearby. They saved my neck, but weren't in time to cut off Roy from getting away. With the truck and old Badger."

"Roy was shooting at you . . ."

"Yes. He had to quit when the hikers came along, or he

wouldn't have gotten back to the truck."

Her clear green eyes were shadowed with anxiety. "You think he's shot Warren by now?"

"No. He wouldn't do that." He wouldn't want the evidence of his bullet in the body; he'd lose the loyalty of his group if they ever found out he'd murdered Warren.

"Who did try to kill him, Lex? Haven't you any idea?"

"I didn't see him. Nor did Warren." This wasn't the time to relay any theory about her father's having a hand in the matter.

"Why was he there—at your hotel? You'd told me you wouldn't be seeing him again."

"He changed his mind. He wanted to give me a warning for Hugo Praeger."

"Hugo Praeger?" She looked around at me in surprise.

"Warren's group plan to assassinate Praeger if he runs for President. Warren dissenting, as you could imagine—"

"My goodness—assassinate—"

"If you've harbored any illusions that Warren's friends are a harmless bunch of do-gooders, forget it."

She shook her head. "I never thought that. A few were just stringing along, with woolly ideas of a better world. I'm sure they dropped by the wayside long since. But Roy Lissing; or Ronald Gore—"

"Ronald!" I grasped her arm. "You've met Ronald?"

"It was awhile ago—"

"And his last name is Gore? Did you tell Sergeant Perreault?"

"No. I hadn't thought of him till just now. He's someone you'd *rather* forget. I don't think he believes in anything—he's in this group of idealists only because he's looking forward to the eventual carnage. There's not an iota of human feeling in him—"

"I gather you didn't get on."

She shuddered. "He used to look at me as if he were imagining me already dead—squashed on the pavement like some-

108

thing that's been stepped on. He loathed anybody who'd ever had a dollar to their name—he dislikes Warren, I'm sure."

So the name Ronald Gore was added to the others in the case and sent out with his description: white male, about thirty-two, five-feet-ten, weight as of four years ago about a hundred and sixty pounds, curly blond hair, blue eyes. "Like an overage cherub," Julie said. "Round face, dimples, round head, with curly hair like a halo. Eyes that look absolutely dead."

We returned to our waiting.

"An apt name—Gore," she said, "considering his personality."

We talked little after that. It could be that a sort of superstition kept us silent: while the mills of the gods are grinding, speak not of what they do.

Julie's nerves were stretched taut, I could see. As mine had been all day.

Time crept by. I could not, though, wish it to speed up—the later it got with no word of Warren, the worse his chances were. If he were not somewhere in a hospital by now—

Sergeant Perreault went home—though he said he'd be back if anything came up.

It was nearly eight. "We'd better have dinner," I said to Julie.

"Oh. Yes—I hadn't thought about food." She consulted the officer on duty and came back with his recommendation of an eating place up the highway.

We walked.

"Not the *Poulet Frit à la Kentucky?*" I asked, reading the sign on a building just ahead. "I didn't realize that was international cuisine."

"No. Beyond." But at least she had smiled, for a change.

We found it; a small café, unpretentious, with cheap pine-paneled walls, plastic-topped tables, and pink ruffled shades—that didn't match anything—on the wall brackets. It was just fine.

We both took the *plat du jour;* some kind of stew—quite

109

good, as was our bottle of wine. Though anything would have tasted marvelous—two hotdogs wasn't much on which to have gotten through the day.

I felt almost as though I were two people—one mourning the tragedy of my friend, the other giddily enjoying the company of the girl I had hankered after for longer than I could remember. And callous as I knew it to be, I was exhilaratingly glad to be me, alive and in good health, instead of Warren, dead or dying.

It was as though she read my mind.

"I thought it was you, of course, who'd been shot." There was something almost accusing in her tone.

"Me?" I'd supposed that if she had even heard of the shooting before today she would intuitively have known the victim was Warren.

"When you didn't come for me at the hotel that morning, I assumed you'd stood me up. Didn't surprise me—" She grimaced. "You scrape me off like a barnacle, nine times out of ten—"

"I *what?*"

But she went on. "So I tried to phone you at the Genève—and got the police. Immediately they wanted to question me; something about a shooting.

" 'What shooting?' I said. And got the impression (this was all in French) that either you'd been shot or you'd disappeared. Or both.

"I hung up. In a panic. I certainly wasn't going to answer questions! The only person I could imagine taking a shot at you would have been one of Warren's revolutionary group. Presumably because you were trying to lure Warren away from them, I suppose. Naturally I couldn't talk to the police. If they knew my connection with Warren—and yours—they'd jump to the conclusion he was involved in the shooting. They'd have been after him like hounds at a fox hunt."

"So you knew nothing about what actually happened."

"Oh, it was all in the papers, and on TV. But the news only bore out what I believed already—I've been visualizing you wounded, possibly abducted as well. Or dead, maybe. And Warren more of a fugitive than ever. This man calling himself Mr. Doe, who had gone up to your room and shot you—"

"Mr. Doe was Warren."

"Yes—I understand that now. But even the newspapers had it wrong. And there was nothing about any third person."

"Not surprising—when even *we* didn't see him."

"Roy Lissing? He's certainly a good candidate. You say Warren had disagreed with the others about assassinating Hugo Praeger. I'd imagine Roy was leading the other faction. There aren't so many in their group that they can stand a division of opinion—Roy could have wanted Warren out of the way."

"Maybe." It was a possibility I'd find easier to live with, I knew, than the premise that I had led a killer to my best friend.

"And now he's in Roy's hands . . ."

"We don't know Roy did it, Julie." I tried to reassure her. "Don't jump to any conclusions. Roy was quite solicitous about him all this time. Only thing was, he wouldn't let us take him to a doctor—it was too risky for their group. He hoped Warren would be all right, you see."

"Oh, sure!"

"He even knocked over a drugstore to get tetracycline and codeine for him."

"Histrionics. Doesn't prove anything."

"God, I've still got his pills . . ." I reached into my slacks pocket for the little aspirin bottle. I set it on the table and looked across to see that tears were silently running down Julie's cheeks.

"You mean all day he hasn't even had them?"

I felt flayed with guilt. "There were more at the farm. They went back there," I said hoarsely. And I remembered the pills

111

and the capsules, abandoned on the floor of the storeroom. "Unless Roy *did* drop him off at some place where he got medical attention."

"First Roy shot him, but he didn't die. So he didn't let him have a doctor, but he didn't die. You think *now* he's going to take him to some nice medical facility so that he can survive?"

"I just don't know, Julie. I don't know." Try as I might, I was unable to lay the conviction that time by now had run out for Warren, if he hadn't reached help.

When we got back to the sûreté post, there was still no news from the search—other than the fact that a boy named Michael Van, who had given the farm as his address, had not shown up for work that day at René's Hamburgers, where he was employed.

There was a message for Julie to call her father at the Regency Hotel in Montreal.

She called, but he wasn't in. She talked to Irwin Kuhn. Irwin was Oliver Thayer's confidential secretary and chief expediter. "They flew up this evening," she said when she'd hung up. In her father's plane, that would have been. "Irwin said Daddy's at Sûreté Headquarters, conferring."

Oliver Thayer would of course go straight to the top echelon of the police—no fooling around out here in the boondocks with sergeants and corporals. He was right. Start at the top if you can.

By midnight there seemed to be no use in hanging out at the sûreté post any longer. Patrol cars had been in and out of the place all evening; officers had trooped up the stairs and down. Communications of all sorts had come in and gone out by radio-phone, but there was no word on the whereabouts of Warren—or the others. Gustave Meunier had gone home at eleven—long after his nighttime relief had come on duty.

There was a motel across from the café where we'd eaten, but its *Vacancy* sign had been turned off hours ago.

"You can perhaps find rooms at the resort," suggested La-vigne, the officer still on duty at the radio-phone, though his glance as it shifted from Julie to me and back again made clear his thought that no more than one room would be needed.

I drove Julie's rental car, and we found the hotel with no trouble—a rugged-looking stone and timber building, on the lines of a huge chalet. From halfway up a hillside it overlooked a good-sized lake which lay dark and quiet in a basin rimmed by mountains.

I wondered whether I'd get past the room clerk in my disreputable condition; my pants and the shirt with the piece torn off didn't just look as if I'd slept in them—I *had* slept in them, and lived in them, ever since Warren and I had escaped from the Hôtel Genève in Montreal. I hadn't bothered then with a jacket, so I had none now. At least I'd succeeded in borrowing a razor from one of the officers during the afternoon.

There was no problem at the hotel—even without luggage. Apparently tourists could be as relaxed and sloppy as they liked. The clerk showed us to our rooms on the second floor—Julie's on the lake side, and mine across the hall and down, with a view of some garbage cans and a parking lot.

I waited until the room clerk would have gone downstairs, and then I went along the hall and knocked on her door.

"You all right?" I asked when she opened it.

"Come in," she said, and I did.

She was in her slip, and she was barefoot—which made her not so tall. I looked down at her—not the Julie I knew, but a girl who was small, soft, and without defenses. Her eyes were huge with fatigue, and luminous—with what? With unshed tears?

I reached for her, and she was warm and real in my arms. I kissed her.

Everything was changed, as of that moment. I didn't have to

113

ask whether she felt the same as I did; I knew.

Time was measureless as her lips moved against mine. Eventually I realized that vertical was going to be an impossible position to maintain—there was an increasingly irresistible appeal belonging to horizontal; so I carried her to the bed.

We curled up there together and looked at each other.

For a long time we said nothing—we smiled, besotted.

"I was sure," she said finally, "that you were going to shut yourself into your room, drop exhausted onto your bed, and sleep soundly all night without giving me another thought."

"Not a chance."

"When did you fall in love with me, Lex?"

"I don't know."

"Oh. That's a terrible thing to say! You don't even remember?" But she remembered the time, the place, and what I was doing when she had first recognized the uniqueness of her feelings for me. Gratifying in the extreme to hear about; I listened greedily. She had realized, she told me, the afternoon I had dug a grave for one of her hamsters and said a service over the body.

"Transference," I diagnosed.

"What?"

"Transference. You transferred your affection for the deceased to the nearest available substitute."

She touched my cheek with her fingers. "I don't think hamsters had anything to do with it."

"And why were you always so cold and standoffish?" I asked her.

"*I* was! *Me?* Oh, Alex Norden! Have you no conception of the maddening, maddening indifference to me that you've displayed all your life? I've needled you, I suppose, so that at least you'd notice me; but you hardly did, at that . . . Every time I

114

made a move in your direction, you went farther into your shell. And I've got *some* pride, you know—"

"So why did you marry Spence Hubbard?" I toyed with a lock of hair that rested on her shoulder. (That horrible, nightmarish time before the annulment . . .)

"That's kind of obvious, isn't it? To blot you out. And at the same time to make you devastatingly sorry. Though I couldn't have it both ways, could I. I'm sure I knew I couldn't."

"Well, I was devastated; that part worked."

She shook her head. "It didn't show."

"And when you were home from Exeter you never noticed how much I hung around?"

"Actually, I sometimes wondered if you weren't half in love with Warren—first cousins, that's not—"

"With *our* shared heredity? That'd be incest. Warren's the same as my brother—always has been . . ." The light faded from her face. "Why don't they call and say they've found him?" She pressed her cheek to mine and slid her arms farther around my neck. I held her and stroked her hair, and caressed her until we both forgot about Warren.

. . . forgot about everything except each other.

8

When I waked, it was long past daylight. She was dressed, and she sat in an armchair by the window, watching me.

"I was afraid I'd get out of the shower and find you gone," she said. "I'd have had no proof then that last night happened."

I might as easily have felt the morning was a dream as well if the leaden memory of Warren hadn't been dragging at my consciousness. I sat up, clasping my knees beneath the sheet.

"Julie—"

She came and seated herself beside me on the bed. I'd meant to ask her if she'd had any second thoughts, any regrets. But I saw that the question wasn't necessary. I kissed her. The sweetness, the joy, were back to back with the contemplation of death, of loss, and we both knew it.

She drew back; looked long at me.

"He's dead," she stated simply.

"Warren's dead? They called?" I glanced wildly at the phone on the nighttable. Surely I couldn't have slept through—

"No, no. There's been no call. That's what I mean. If he hasn't reached a hospital by now . . ."

I phoned the sûreté post and talked to Corporal Meunier. No news.

Julie called her father. A lot was being done, according to Oliver, but as yet with no results.

We breakfasted at the hotel, on a terrace overlooking the lake. The sky was bright, the sun shone. Above our heads flags snapped in the morning breeze—the maple leaf of Canada, and the blue and white fleur-de-lis of Quebec. A small plane circled over the mountains across from us, and below, boats raced over the water. A single water skier kept falling into the drink.

Not for us the lighthearted summer pursuits of the tourists breakfasting around us; we were still claimed by yesterday's trauma. The vacation setting, even the vast beguiling landscape stretching to the humpbacked blue peaks in the distance, served only to underline the ephemeral quality of the few hours, now drawing to a close, that we would have been able to spend here.

We were not in a hurry; the police didn't need us at this moment, and Oliver Thayer was undoubtedly making sufficient waves at headquarters in Montreal. But soon we must leave.

We were quiet, and we looked at each other a lot.

We went into Emilion on our way to the post and bought me a new shirt, socks, undershorts, and a razor and shaving cream. We checked in then at the post, and as before Dubreuil passed me on to Meunier, and we ended up conferring with Sergeant Perreault.

"They would like you to come into Montreal," Perreault told me. "There are some questions to be asked about the shooting of Mr. Thayer at the Hôtel Genève . . ."

I shaved in the officers' quarters, and changed my clothes, and we headed down the autoroute in Julie's car. I drove; most of the way one-handed. We were quiet, still, as we'd been at breakfast.

She asked one question, though.

"Didn't Warren's friends have any theory about who shot him?"

I told her.

She leaned forward in her seat, so that she could look more

117

fully into my face. "Why, that's insane!"

"Well, it's what they believe."

Her eyes narrowed. "They don't know my father, of course
. . ." I didn't think knowing him would have changed their
opinion—except to strengthen it. "People like my father don't
do such things."

"Since Watergate, people will believe anything of anyone."

She shook her head. "But when Warren's his own nephew!"
She had disposed of the accusation in her own mind as impossible, without its occurring to her to ask my opinion of it.

I left Julie, with her rental car, at the Regency and went on
by taxi to the address Sergeant Perreault had given me—a huge,
very modern building near the river. Here I talked to Sergeant
Talbot, one of the specialists who had come out to Emilion the
day before. He was a square-built man, fairly tall, with a pock-
marked face and a quick, dazzlingly white smile.

"I have a preliminary report on the bullet you took out of
Thayer. It's a thirty-two. Though we hope to learn more than
that by the time they've finished with it in the lab."

"No gun was recovered at the hotel?"

"No. The municipal police have been working on the case,
naturally. So far they have located no suspects—other than
perhaps you."

"Me?" Talbot's very modern office seemed all at once oppres-
sively official.

"It was you whom Mr. Thayer came to see. There is no
known connection between Mr. Thayer and anyone else who
was in the Hôtel Genève. You could have quarreled, you shot
him, then forced him to accompany you out of the building."

In desperate earnest I leaned forward. "But he's my friend!"

He flashed the dazzling smile. "So we are now informed. But
the police did not have that information until yesterday. The
story you told Sergeant Perreault has been passed on to the
Montreal police. And it would indeed seem unlikely that you

118

would shoot a man and then spend days trying to save his life."

"Mr. Oliver Thayer, also, would—"

"Yes, I have spoken with Mr. Thayer, and the Montreal police have talked with him since. I doubt that there will any longer be a problem of your being a suspect." So why had he deliberately given me the opposite impression, in the beginning? A little cat and mouse?

"On what happened out in the mountains, now—" he went on. "As of this morning we believe we may have located the garage where this man Roy Lissing was employed. A mechanic named Rob Martin fits Lissing's description. If it is the same man—we are not sure yet. There is some confusion about the address the garage owner has for him; it is so illegible on his records it cannot be read."

"I'm sure he's not working there now—"

"No. He came in yesterday morning to collect his pay—he said he was quitting."

"What time yesterday?"

"Ten o'clock or a little later. After he had left you—if it was Lissing. Before the roadblocks were set up."

In any case, he was gone now.

Next I spoke with the R.C.M.P. man I had met the day before—O'Neill. He wanted to come along when I went with the Montreal police to the Genève. I was to point out for them the exact spot where Warren had been when he was struck.

"Here." I stood in the corridor, close to the stairwell. It was as near as I could make it to the place Warren had reached when I heard the shot and he stumbled.

"Facing how?" asked Lambert, the officer from the Montreal force. O'Neill leaned on the railing at the head of the stairs and watched.

"You saw him at the moment he was struck?"

"Yes. I had come out of my room and into the corridor to meet him." I walked toward the rear, in the direction of the room I had occupied. "I was here."

Both officers followed; O'Neill—tall, short-necked, with huge shoulders, a broken nose, and graying red hair; Lambert —soft-spoken, middle-sized, and dark-complexioned, with heavy-lidded protuberant eyes.

They stood where I had stood. Years ago, it seemed now, that I had been here and Warren had come.

"Did you see anyone else?" Lambert asked.

"No one. Only Warren Thayer."

"No movement? A door opening or closing?"

"No."

"Did you hear anything?"

"Nothing but the sound of the shot. I believe I called out to him just before that, so if there was any slight noise at that moment I probably wouldn't have heard it."

We walked back to the head of the stairs.

"Did Thayer tell you he saw or heard anyone?" O'Neill asked.

"He told me he did not."

He scanned the hallway; turned questioningly to Lambert. "You've found no one yet who saw anything suspicious? Someone on the stairs, or—"

"No one appears to have seen anything. The maid for this floor was in the linen closet. Any of the guests along here who were present in the hotel at the time were in their rooms with the doors closed. All of them must have heard the shot, but those who recognized it for what it was were afraid to open their doors. By the time the first of them decided the firing was over and looked out, there was no one here in the hall, not even Thayer or Mr. Norden."

I wondered. "Did anyone come into the hotel just after Warren, and follow him up the stairs?" I was thinking of Roy, at odds with Warren over the Praeger issue; Roy who knew, because Eve had said she told him, that Warren and I were in communication—and who disapproved.

120

"The desk clerk saw no one. Though he says that he was talking on the telephone and might not have noticed. In any case no such person came down again, because only registered guests of the hotel were found to be—"

I broke in. "Someone had gone down the fire escape before Warren and I did. The bottom section was already lowered when we reached it."

"Ah," said Lambert. "We did not know that, but we thought it possible that our man had left that way."

O'Neill started for the rear of the building. "From which rooms is the fire escape accessible?"

Lambert and I went with him.

"It's reached not only from the rooms along the back, but also from a window in a hallway." At the rear of the main corridor, instead of turning left toward the room I had had, we turned right. Off this hall, a little way on to the left, was another, dead ending at a window which served to light a dreary cul-de-sac. "There's this one, and there's one like it on the floor below."

Outside the grimy glass was the iron railing of the fire escape. The window was open about four inches at the bottom.

O'Neill tested it, and the sash moved upwards with a complaining squeal. "Was this open that day?"

"The way you saw it. A few inches."

"How about the one on the floor below?"

"Open about the same, when we examined it. And it slides up and down quite easily." Lambert turned to face the taller officer at his side. "As it happens, we have a possible suspect now. A man who was staying on the floor below. Whether we'll be able to locate him is another matter—he has not been seen since before the shooting."

"You believe that he was in the hotel at the time?"

"The woman who occupied the next room saw him as she returned from the lavatory—his door was open a crack. But by the time my men got here, he was gone, his room empty."

121

"Had he any luggage?"

"A small case, which he must have taken with him—like an attaché case, perhaps. And he left without paying his bill."

"When did he check in?" I asked Lambert.

"The night before Thayer was shot. Late."

"After eleven-forty?" That had been the time when the desk clerk had handed me Warren's telephoned message—I'd glanced at the clock on the wall.

"Yes. After eleven-forty. It was a few minutes before twelve."

There was a hollow, sickish feeling in my stomach. "I had thought it possible that someone who wanted to get at Warren could have trailed me when I came back to the hotel." I explained how careful I had been, until that evening, to cover my tracks—for the reason that Warren wouldn't agree to meet me if he thought the police could be tailing me.

"And who do you think might want to 'get at' Thayer, as you put it?" O'Neill's washed-out blue eyes studied me intently.

"I don't know." To name Oliver Thayer in a hypothetical plot would be preposterous! A man of his reputation? The victim's uncle? There wasn't a shred of credibility to such a suggestion. "I only know that unless this was a completely random, motiveless shooting, whoever tried to kill him must either have followed me here that night, or followed Warren the next morning. This isn't a place he had ever been in his life."

"I doubt that it was a motiveless killing," said Lambert. "It would seem that Harris, the suspect I mentioned, could have been lying in wait. He asked for a room near the stairs. The reason he gave was that he'd been caught in a hotel fire once; never again. Perhaps he wanted to watch the stairs? He could also watch the street and the hotel entrance from his room; it's at the front."

"American? Or Canadian?" O'Neill inquired.

"He gave his address as Boston." Lambert's heavy-lidded eyes blinked. "John J. Harris, Commonwealth Avenue. Naturally we have inquired, and there is no such person at the

122

number he put down. I'm sure the name is false as well as the address."

"He might have stayed at the Queen Elizabeth under that name," I suggested. "If he followed me, it was from there. And if he'd been trying before that to keep an eye on me, hoping to find Warren, the Queen Elizabeth was where I stayed before I came to the Hôtel Genève."

"I'll find out," said Lambert.

"What did this man look like?"

"About five-feet-seven, slight build, dark hair, somewhat sharp features, forty to forty-five years old."

Definitely not Roy Lissing—not tall enough. "Clean-shaven?"

"Yes." No way had it been Roy.

"We've got a mass of fingerprints from that room—probably none of them the ones we want. There were two from the fire escape window on that floor, the one from the corridor, but they belonged to the maid." Lambert had turned back now to the officer from the R.C.M.P.

"The maid for that floor didn't see anything that morning?" O'Neill asked.

"No. She was off sick."

We went down a flight, to where we'd left the hotel manager pacing up and down hoping for our imminent departure. He let us into the room where a man calling himself John J. Harris had spent a night.

One could observe the stairs excellently from room 217; one could also see every person—if one wished to—who came in or out the entrance to the hotel.

A man with an alias. A man who had disappeared on Saturday morning down the fire escape. A man who had probably worn gloves so as to leave no prints.

Julie had moved from her hotel to the Regency, to be with her father, I found out when late in the afternoon I myself again registered at the Queen Elizabeth. She'd left a message for me.

I had had to reclaim my luggage from the Montreal police department, who on the strength of the spectacular bloodstains in my room at the Genève, had impounded it. They also had my car, which had been towed away and examined by the police lab technicians after it had been discovered near Warren's apartment. When the proper phone calls had been made and the necessary forms signed, I was able to take away with me what was mine.

A tip the size of a bribe got my long-packed jacket and a pair of slacks pressed by the hotel valet service in less than half an hour, and feeling again presentable, I went over to the Regency.

Uncle Oliver had taken a very large suite—about half a floor. Julie let me into the opulent foyer, with its huge gilt-framed mirrors, dark oil paintings and a crystal chandelier.

I'd been nervous before I came—as unstrung when I waited at her door as I had ever been at the prospect of being with Warren's glacial cousin.

I needn't have worried. The polarized gaze of lovers drew us together at once, and touch reaffirmed what we'd said to each other last night.

We went into the living room—large, carpeted in sculptured gold and furnished with a combination of French antiques and modern down-filled sofas and chairs. There was a much larger crystal chandelier and a white marble fireplace. On either side of the fireplace arched floor-length windows, swathed across the top and down the sides with curtains and overdrapes, gave on a terrace beyond.

We went out on the terrace.

From the moment I'd stepped into the foyer, I had known that she was waiting to tell me something—some kind of bad news.

"What is it?" I asked, holding her hand. I had no need of the twelve-floor drop from the terrace balustrade to make my head swim.

Her lips thinned as she pressed them against each other. "You know the little bottle with Warren's pills that you showed me? I kept it—"

"I remember you did."

"I was curious, so I took them to a pharmacist this afternoon. The codeine pills are all right—the white ones. But the others —the pink capsules . . . You said they were tetracycline?"

I nodded, dumbly.

"They're gelatin capsules. Nothing more than that. For people who have weak fingernails."

I stared at her. "You're sure?" The picture of Roy was before me; Roy holding out the bottles, one in each hand, to Eve. He'd looked so pleased with himself, I remembered.

"Yes, I'm sure! The pharmacist told me these couldn't be tetracycline. There's a tetracycline capsule put out by Squibb that looks very similar—pink, like the ones in that bottle, though not the same shade. But the real ones have the name Squibb printed on each capsule. A pharmacist can tell the difference just by looking. I took the bottle to Sûreté Headquarters then, and it was turned over to the lab. Gelatin—I waited for the verdict."

"That was murder!" I said slowly. "Not just a mistake, because the bottle Roy brought those in was the right one—the large pharmacist's bottle; labeled. He'd have had to dump out the tetracycline and replace it."

Had it been Roy in the beginning, then, who had tried to kill him? John J. Harris could be a man who was afraid of hotel fires, and who had left without paying his bill—without ever in his life laying eyes on Warren Thayer.

It must have been another hour before Oliver Thayer came to join us on the terrace, accompanied by Irwin Kuhn. I'd met Irwin before, once or twice, when he'd come to Frances's house on some errand. He was a pleasant-mannered man who I understood had nerves of steel and a backbone to match. People who

125

thought they could get around him, could use him to obtain some favor from Oliver Thayer, had always come up against a nasty surprise. He didn't give an inch, and in dealing with people he got what he wanted—not for himself but for Thayer. His very pleasant, easy-going manner was part of the equipment for his job.

"Well, Alex!" Oliver came across the terrace to where we sat between two potted trees. I rose and we shook hands. Kuhn, in his wake, nodded to me and seated himself on a bench next to the parapet.

Oliver, too, sat down. "It's late to thank you, I know, for all you've done." There was a gleam of warmth in the eyes, deep-set in the rugged face.

"I'm afraid there's nothing to thank me for. It's been a fiasco."

"Not a fiasco—you did the best that could be done. What's happened—well, that's something else entirely." He hunched his elegantly tailored shoulders. "It would seem you chanced to arrive here just when Warren's group had split into two camps over assassinating Hugo Praeger. Apparently Warren was odd man out, and one or more of his comrades decided to get rid of him. Isn't that how it must be?"

"But what I can't forget is that I may have precipitated their taking such a step. Roy Lissing could have been afraid he'd leak their plans to me. As he did."

Oliver Thayer put out a hand and laid it on my knee. "Don't torment yourself over it, Alex. Warren was bound to come to grief one way or another, in this thing. Nothing that's happened was any fault of yours." To my relief, he took his hand away.

"I've talked with Praeger, by the way. He's most grateful for your warning. I don't care for Hugo's brand of politics myself —*much* too far left. The man's brilliant, but he should stick to news analysis and being a TV glamor boy, not turn his hand to government." He smiled; his eyes glowed again with perhaps amusement. "Of course with the power he wields as an opinion-maker, he's not a man to cross—a good one, in fact, to have done a favor."

Whichever of the two had called which, Oliver Thayer had been quite ready and more than happy, it was clear, to take credit for the warning to Praeger with which he'd had nothing to do. Perhaps he even believed that he *was* responsible for uncovering the plot against Praeger's life, but it seemed more likely that the assumption of the role of savior had been calculated. I'd heard my father say that Oliver Thayer succeeded in the business world as much by adroitly using his enemies as by finding support among his allies. I could believe it; he had managed now to put in his debt a man who politically was his natural foe. And Praeger, as publisher of *The New York Evening Standard,* would be a good man anytime to have in one's corner.

Drinks were served from a tray brought out to the terrace from a bar in the living room. While Oliver quizzed me on the details of the last few days, his valet dispensed the cocktails, each from its individual one-serving bottle, with water added, or soda, as needed.

Oliver and Irwin Kuhn offered comments on my narrative, from time to time, and Julie sat beside me, listening, her head turned away as she gazed out at the cityscape around us.

I was conscious of a phone which rang, now and again, and was answered, in some room within the suite. Twice an earnest-looking girl in a navy dress with white piping came to fetch Irwin away to deal with a call.

What a neat person Irwin Kuhn was, I thought—immaculate, with not a wrinkle in his light gray suit or snow-white shirt; his tie impeccably knotted; not a hair on his shining blond head out of place. Warren had always sworn Irwin wore a hairpiece—that years ago he'd had a sizeable bald spot on top that was no longer in evidence.

"The newspapers," he explained when he came back the second time.

127

"They were lucky to get what they did out of me at the airport last night." Oliver frowned in impatience. "That will have to do for a while."

"There's a news photographer waiting for you in the street outside the hotel, the management tells me—"

"So we'll eat upstairs. I'd planned to anyway."

Upstairs turned out to be the rooftop restaurant—famous in the city for its French cuisine. Only the three of us went—Julie, her father and me. Irwin Kuhn said he'd get something from room service; he was tied to the phone.

"Have you given him up?" Julie had asked me as we waited in the suite's foyer for her father, who was delayed by a call from New York. Almost as though she thought my opinion could make some difference in what had become of Warren.

After the news about the pink capsules I couldn't see much to hope for. "We can pray that miracles still happen."

At dinner, however, she shut away her worry and became animated in a way I had never seen her before. "What's come over you, Julie?" her father asked, amused. She sat between the two of us, looking almost ethereal in the subdued light of the black-walled room. "Have you gotten secretly engaged or something?"

I reached out and put my hand over hers, where it rested on the table. "Yes, she has. It was quite sudden."

"Ah, it's you, Alex!" There seemed to be no reservations in his smile. Indeed, he was probably relieved—knowing, as he did, all the essential things about me. My family was suitable —that was what mattered: they were from his own social set, my father had a seat on the stock exchange, and my bloodlines were as good as his own—possibly better.

I didn't hear him order it, but the champagne arrived quite promptly; in honor of the occasion. It did not take long for me to feel properly welcomed as a member of the family.

"Christine will be delighted . . ." He said this because he felt he should, I suppose, but with a watchful eye on his daughter.

"Christine will not give a damn one way or the other, and you know it. Except that she'll be rid of me for good, and she should enjoy that."

"You've hardly been in the house enough even to *know* my wife, dear child—and we've been married twenty years." He spoke without rancor, but there was a definite reproach in his voice.

"Daddy, it wasn't all on my side, you know. She couldn't stand me. She can hardly even abide Richie, and he's *hers!*"

"Well, they've had their differences. Christine has never understood Richie as I do. Boys will be boys, we've always heard, and young men do sow wild oats; but it's been hard for Christine to realize those things are only phases in growing up." His face darkened. "Not like this revolutionary kick of Warren's. What he's put the family through, blackening the name of Thayer! I've been ashamed even to—"

Julie cut in, her eyes bright with anger. "Daddy! You mustn't say things like that about Warren! When he's somewhere dying? Warren's more my brother than your dear Richie has ever been! You speak of blackening the name of Thayer—if Richie and Mark Theobald—"

Oliver grasped his daughter's wrist with a force that stopped her words in her throat. "*Nothing* happened with Richie and —I'd even forgotten the boy's name. He was unfortunate in his choice of friends, that's all. And the episode is closed, you understand?"

She looked at her father in chilly defiance. "If nothing happened, is it worth breaking my arm?"

He let go of it and patted her hand. "You mustn't speak irresponsibly as you did. I suppose you take for granted the fact that you belong to one of the great families of America—but it's a thing you must never forget for a moment. You do not even *jokingly* detract from what the Thayer family stands for."

She flashed a look at me—perhaps for moral support. She did not, I'm sure, see his incredible pomposity for what it was.

With a little smile she looked him in the eyes. "Enrollment might fall off at the Thayer School of Medicine? Or attendance at the art museum? Or are you planning to go into politics, like Rocky?" She sucked in her cheeks. "All right. I'll go along with the Shinto Thayers."

"Sorry to have made such an issue of it." He was speaking to me. He made a deprecating gesture with his hand. "I'm on edge—we all are, I'm sure—with this unresolved situation concerning Warren."

"Let's talk about something else—can't we?" Julie appealed to both of us.

"Of course." Her father deliberately changed his mood to something bordering on gaiety. (How could he do that so fast? I wondered.) "We'll talk about you. Alex and I will, at any rate."

It was as though we'd turned a corner and were on another street. No disagreements. Dinner became a delightful party. Oliver Thayer was his most charming. Although there may have been an edge of hysteria to Julie's high spirits, the effect was dazzling to behold. Even I became talkative, which I usually am not.

For much of the time I watched Julie interacting with her father, and I came to understand her better simply from what I observed that night. As again and again she hung on his words, and then gave him a snappy riposte, I thought of the little girl with the icy poise, the scornful glance—a little girl who had shuttled back and forth between the two halves of her family, with no permanent home to call her own. Emotionally she'd been an orphan.

She had lavished affection on the dogs and cats at her Uncle Stuart's house; on the ponies and horses that had been hers. But with people . . . Her love for her father was something that pride had required her to conceal—since he had betrayed her by marrying the hated Christine. Coldness and indifference had been her weapons of choice—the only warmth she'd ever shown

130

having been the heat of anger where her stepmother was concerned. Even her relationship with her Aunt Fran had been flawed. Frances was more than an aunt, but she wasn't her mother; and though Julie took refuge in the house of her aunt and uncle, her place was not really with them but at her father's home.

It was painful now to remember how Warren and I had brushed her off, when she'd tried to tag along. So many times. "No girls. Just me and Lex are doing this." A long time ago, that had been.

If only I had understood her before . . .

We had left the restaurant and were heading for the bank of elevators when we met Irwin Kuhn in the wide black-carpeted hall.

"Some news from the police," he said to Oliver. "I was coming to find you."

I think we all froze.

"Yes, what is it?"

"They'd like you to come to the Sûreté Headquarters. You and Julie. They have a watch which they believe is Warren's."

"Where—where did they get it?" Julie's hand was at her throat.

"It turned up in Toronto. A man pawned it there this morning. This afternoon the pawnbroker read in the paper about the search for Warren, and called the police. Took till now to get the watch here to Montreal."

Julie had turned, white-faced, to me. "Warren would *never* have pawned it!" And to her father, "It's the watch I gave him, with his initials. No one could mistake it—"

I put my arm around her, and she turned inward to press her forehead against my shoulder. Her voice was muffled. "He wouldn't have let them take it off him, either. If he was alive."

I was looking over her head at her father. "He's dead, then," I heard him murmur, very low. One corner of his mouth

131

quirked up in an involuntary smile.

People do smile, in a manner they cannot help, when they hear of a death. Sometimes. But there was something besides in Oliver's rugged, handsome face—it was like a flash of triumph.

He was glad. Glad.

But then he had never liked Warren, had he.

It was Warren's watch. I held her hand while she identified it; looked over her shoulder at the whirring, twinkling movement of its parts in the see-through case. There was something ironic, something cruel and terrible in the fact that though its owner, wherever he was, no longer breathed and his heart was stilled, the watch still ticked and moved like a live thing.

Oliver came to join us. He'd been talking to one of the sûreté officers in the corridor.

"Warren's?" he asked. Julie nodded.

"According to the Toronto police, the man who pawned it answers pretty closely to the description of Roy Lissing."

Naturally.

"We can reclaim the watch when the police have finished with it?" Oliver asked of the officer who had it in his charge.

"Of course, Mr. Thayer. It will be returned to you."

We threaded our way through the corridors and out of the building. I led Julie, who walked as though she were blind, out through the entrance and into the warm night. Almost overhead, as we made our way into the parking lot, one of the highway bridges which crossed the St. Lawrence loomed against the sky.

I wondered. Had he stopped breathing all on his own? Or had Roy Lissing expedited his transition from life to oblivion . . . ?

Part Three

9

Oliver and Christine Thayer insisted on giving an elaborate party to announce our engagement; not at once—it would not have been suitable, Oliver said, to dramatize the family in such a manner too soon after the spate of news about Warren which had been in the papers. So the party was to be in September.

Upon our return from Canada, Julie had had to leave at once for Mexico, where she was scheduled to cover several of the newer resorts for the travel pages of *Savoir-faire,* the fashion magazine for which she worked. I counted the days till she would return.

And I received my first telephone call via satellite—from my parents in Hong Kong; perhaps they'd better cancel their trip and come home—

"Why?" I said. I not only was fine, I was engaged—and they would be back in plenty of time for the wedding.

Well, if I was sure . . .

I went regularly to see Frances, who had taken the news about Warren quite badly. She looked more fragile than ever, and the shadows under her eyes were like bruises made by a fist.

"It's bad enough, what you've told me, Lex." (Though I'd spared her the more harrowing details.) "But the inconclusiveness—not to know. That's worse. One minute I tell myself he's dead, the next I'm convinced he's still alive somewhere. When he's been a wanted fugitive, you know, that would be the perfect way to become safe: let everyone think you're dead."

"He couldn't have survived, Frances. I saw him and I know." It was kinder to tell her that than to let her go on nursing an impossible hope.

When an old friend wrote inviting her for a visit at her chateau near Antibes, John the butler and I packed her off.

At Hugo Praeger's request, I went to see him.

He'd phoned me himself, and I went over to his apartment on Park Avenue—a handsome, comfortable place furnished in a starkly modern style which served perfectly as a background for the things he'd acquired in his years as a foreign correspondent—before he'd started his own newspaper.

I'd never met Praeger, but his face, his voice, his assured, distinctive manner were familiar to me from his television appearances. He had been a favorite guest, the past few years, on panel or talk shows.

He was a more somber-looking man than I had imagined. I saw at once that the vibrancy he projected on TV was something that took a lot of energy and directed effort to produce. Not, I mean, that he would have been insincere when he leaned toward the cameras or his TV host and took his audience into his confidence, charming and mesmerizing them into seeing issues as he saw them; but he was "on" at those times, as is an actor when he is before the public.

He was tall—taller than I am, which made him six-four or more. Even his hair had vitality, curling up exuberantly from his forehead—light brown, with no hint of gray. Hawklike features, and greenish eyes which reminded me of Warren's.

"You went through quite an ordeal, I understand," he said when he'd shaken my hand and seated me in a great overstuffed chair beneath a pair of Japanese paintings on silk; on the opposite wall was an old and ornate pictorial map of Paris.

"It was Warren Thayer who really went through an ordeal," I said, "and then didn't survive."

Soberly, Praeger nodded. "Such a waste. And he was a boy of such capability, such promise. I met him once—at his father's funeral. I knew Stuart Thayer quite well."

I wondered how many men would remember having met a fifteen-year-old boy at a funeral that had taken place twelve years before.

"The tragedy of the Vietnam War," he went on, "for a whole segment of the youth of this country simply cannot be measured: what it did to the ones who went, and the ones who refused to go—and to the ones who may not have been required to go but who took up the cudgels in defense, as they saw it, of their entire generation and of the peace of the world. A terrible thing."

He offered me a cigarette. I refused and he took one, tapped it on the slate top of the coffee table, and lit it. "But then I didn't ask you here to listen to a lecture. Or a political speech.

"I wish to thank you for the warning I was given of a threat against my life. Not least, I want to thank you for the way you handled the matter. There's been no publicity on the subject; not a rumor has reached the press. Of that I'm glad. Only the Canadian Mounties and the F.B.I. were given this information you had, I understand."

"That's right."

"And your friend Warren said the assassination attempt would come *only* if and when I declare myself a candidate for the presidency?"

"Yes. Unless the group should decide to change its schedule —that's always possible."

"I don't think they'll jump the gun. There's much greater symbolic value in killing off a presidential candidate than an ordinary newsman."

That's objectivity, I thought—seeing in the prospect of his own murder the issues outweighing the event!

"You're going to run, Mr. Praeger?"

"Yes, indeed! On a third-party ticket."

"I hoped you would. I'd like to help in your campaign—"

"Thanks." He grinned, showing furrows in his cheeks and fine wrinkles around his eyes. "I'll need all the help I can get. The Republicans already have their candidate, of course, in President Ford. And neither party will put together a platform I'd run on—even if they'd have me. My fund-raising campaign's already under way. In a couple of months, perhaps, I'll be ready to make my official announcement. Late September. Or October."

He'd asked me for cocktails, actually. Some other people came, and I met a few of his backers. They were a high-powered group.

But it was the man himself who mattered; not the forces that might rally around him. I left feeling that whether he were elected or not, Praeger's was a voice in this country that was irreplaceable. It would be a loss beyond compare if it were stilled by an assassin's bullet.

I conferred—while Julie was still away—with the F.B.I. in their offices on East Sixty-ninth Street.

The man I talked to there was George Cavanaugh—whom I'd never have picked as F.B.I. He seemed very much an office type: outgoing, brisk. I couldn't imagine him with a gun in his hand.

He told me that the ejected shell from the weapon which had shot Warren had been found belatedly on the stairs at the Hôtel Genève. It had fallen into a crevice between the carpet and the wall.

"So we know that the weapon was a thirty-two automatic."

"Then it wasn't Roy Lissing who shot him," I said. "He had a revolver, not an automatic."

"Well, some of these people have arsenals. But the police know anyhow that it couldn't have been Lissing. His identity as Rob Martin, a mechanic employed at a garage in Sainte Agathe, has been confirmed. The morning Thayer was shot— a Saturday—Lissing was at work. The garage is open Saturday mornings, closes at noon. Lissing got a phone call that day— must have been the one about Warren Thayer's being wounded. But the garage owner says he worked his full stint. Eight to twelve."

That explained part of the long wait, I thought. Two hours before he had come for Warren.

"And on the Monday," Cavanaugh went on, "this fellow known as Rob Martin showed up midmorning and demanded his pay—he was quitting.

"It was a couple of days before anyone discovered the license plates missing from a wreck that had been towed in. It was sitting there back of the garage, and Lissing must have taken the plates that day. Explaining, I guess, the neat vanishing act of his panel truck from under the noses of the Canadian patrol cars."

He went on to give me more, then, of the information that slowly was accumulating as a result of investigation begun in Canada and followed through in Washington.

The sûreté specialists had lifted dozens of fingerprints in the farmhouse. Roy's, certainly, and mine. Warren's and Eve's; though neither of them had ever been fingerprinted, their prints were matched to the ones from their apartment in Montreal. A small carton—empty—addressed to Evelyn Roberts supplied a last name for the girl who had lived with Warren; if it was really her name.

Gary was identified as Gary Bell. Arrested in California during some student violence and charged with destruction of campus property, he'd been fined and let off. Later he had been picked up in connection with the fire-bombing of a police station, but nothing had been proven and he was released.

Mick was Michael Evans. He had twice served time for possession of drugs—marijuana and hashish. He had been arrested and served time for burglary. We was wanted for armed robbery and assault with intent to kill, in connection with the robbery of a liquor store. In the province of Quebec, he had been employed, from the previous fall till his disappearance in July, at a hamburger stand located on the highway not far from the farm, and the name he'd gone by had been Michael Van.

I identified pictures of Gary and Mick, and updated the ones they had of Roy Lissing with a description of his beard.

Lucia, like Eve, had apparently never been fingerprinted. Nor was anything found with her name on it, first or last. Nothing was known about her other than the description I'd given.

Ronald Gore. His name was known in various quarters; it had cropped up, over a period of years, as that of a man on the fringes of trouble. Back when there'd been so much college unrest, the name Ronald Gore had several times appeared in the pages of reports on the investigations—after the fact—of the eruption of actual violence. Yet in none of these cases was Gore enrolled in the college where the trouble had occurred. If the police anywhere had ever had Gore in their hands, it had not been under that name. So there were no prints on file for him, no photographs.

And no one had heard of him lately.

I left the F.B.I. offices feeling disconcerted. I had preferred to believe it had been Roy, even in the beginning, who had wanted Warren dead. Roy who had taken the shot at him.

Ronald Gore, maybe? He'd been somewhere within range, since he and Roy had had a face-to-face conference a couple of days later.

The other possibility was the one that depressed me . . . Oliver . . . *He sent you,* Eve had said, *to ferret him out so he could be killed* . . . There was the recollection, too, of my father-in-law-to-be standing in front of a huge arrangement of white flowers displayed against a black wall in the Regency

Hotel and saying, *He's dead, then.* With the little smile and the flash of triumph that followed it.

Early in August, Julie returned from Mexico. We'd be married, we decided, the week before Thanksgiving.

Julie worked with a police artist on a sketch of Ronald Gore. The drawing was completed, but she was far from satisfied with it. Though she was sure she'd recognize him immediately if she saw him again, it had been so long since they had met that she couldn't get the features right for the sketch.

The picture was turned in anyway, for what help it might be.

"I should go to work for Hugo Praeger as a campaign assistant," she said to me. "If Ronald's the one planning the assassination, I might spot him. Surely he'll make a study of Praeger's routine?"

"If Praeger's going to be shot at, I don't want you anywhere *near* him!" I was vehement on the subject.

And in the meantime nothing happened (that we heard of, anyway) in the search for Warren's comrades.

We spent all our free time together—much of it at my apartment, high above the East River. Every day we met for lunch, and in the evening Julie often cooked dinner for us, on my almost unused stove. Or we went out, some evenings, to restaurants—where we sat side by side, and I could hold her hand, or across from each other and I could look at her.

I remember that time as a kind of honeymoon. Short and very sweet. Short because she soon had to take off again on her job, this time to Europe.

Time dragged while she was away. There was one new development in the search for Ronald Gore. Cavanaugh phoned to tell me of it. It was known now that Gore had flown to Montreal from New York City on the day Roy had conferred with him. And he had flown back that night.

Since there was no record of his having crossed into Canada

a few days previously, he would seem to have been on the American side of the border the morning Warren had been shot.

A couple of days after this conversation I got a call from Oliver.

"Can you drop over to my office, Lex?"

So on my lunch hour I dropped over.

I went through the heavy glass doors into the glass building. Took the sleek and shiny elevator to the seventeenth floor. Haunted by my last visit here two months ago.

Noiselessly the elevator doors opened and I went on into the spacious reception area beyond which lay Oliver's office.

There was the wall of gray glass, this one looking across the side street; the comfortable arrangement of easy chairs—all empty—for visitors; the free-form glass table, supporting a single massive ashtray; the forest of palms and rubber plants near the glass.

No one was waiting—there was only the receptionist at her desk near Oliver's door. And for the first time since I'd seen him on that other day I'd been here, I thought of the man who had been waiting ahead of me.

A thin man with a gray crew cut, I remembered. A man who had stared after me when I left—resentfully, I'd thought, because I'd been given preference in getting in to see Oliver Thayer. When I had first come in, the man had been bent over some papers, his face half averted. When I'd left, he'd been blowing his nose into his handkerchief—but I remembered his small black eyes.

On this recollection was suddenly imposed another—that of the man who had stood directly behind me in the elevator at the Queen Elizabeth the morning I'd received Warren's letter. A small, thin man with pointed features and carefully combed black hair. A wig? Once the two remembered images had slid together, I couldn't get them apart.

140

"Mr. Norden, isn't it?" the girl was saying. "You can go right in."

"Thank you." My pulse rate had picked up as though I had an illness. *Five-feet-seven, slight build, dark hair, somewhat sharp features, forty to forty-five years old.* That was the description of John J. Harris, who had given a false address and had asked for a room by the stairs at the Hôtel Genève and had departed without paying his bill.

I went on into Oliver's office.

"Lex. It's good to see you!" He was shaking my hand.

I was barely able to pay attention to what he was saying, even though it was about Julie, to whom he'd talked on the phone the night before. She was in Copenhagen. "We finalized plans for the announcement party—she'll be home just in time for it."

"Well, it wouldn't be much of a party without her, would it."

He turned to the marble slab desk behind him and picked up a box.

"The police have finally sent this down from Montreal," he said. Intuition told me what it was even before he opened the lid and took out Warren's watch. "Julie says Warren would have wanted you to have it."

I didn't want it. I didn't think I could bear to wear it and look at it two dozen times a day. "It should go to Frances."

"It would only upset Frances to have it. She's in bad enough shape now, without being presented with his personal effects."

"You don't think it would upset *me?*" There must have been resentment in my voice, because he looked at me oddly and shrugged.

"Suit yourself, Lex. He was *your* friend . . ."

I hesitated, feeling that if I took the watch I would have made some kind of commitment. "All right."

He handed it to me, and I put it in my pocket.

"Can you have lunch with me? I'm going over to my club. I'd be so glad—"

"Thank you, I can't," I said in almost a panic. "I'm meeting an old school friend downtown for lunch."

"Sorry—we'll do it another time."

On my way out I saw again, in my mind's eye, the man with the gray crew cut and the black eyes. He'd been somewhat older than forty to forty-five; but a black wig could have given him a younger appearance . . . ?

The "old school friend" had been nonexistent. I wolfed a couple of hamburgers on my way back to the office. And when I got there I took out of my pocket the gift that Julie had given her cousin Warren. Its parts were turning, and oscillating, just as before. It seemed alive.

I took off the watch I wore—an Accutron—and slipped Warren's, with the expandable bracelet, onto my wrist.

As I had guessed, wearing it was a kind of commitment. I was committed to the unmasking of the man who had caused the death of my best friend.

Even if that man was Julie's father?

142

10

Julie came back from Europe two days before the Thayers' big party. Though I met her flight at Kennedy, it had been delayed for hours, and I barely got to see her before delivering her to Frances's apartment in a state of exhaustion.

"Daddy's expecting me out at the house tomorrow," she said as we waited for John to unbolt and unlock the door from within. It was nearly five A.M.—midmorning according to the European time by which she'd lived the day before.

"I'll not see you till the party, then?"

She almost fell asleep while I was kissing her good night.

The engagement party gave me a feeling of time dislocated, people displaced. I was in Warren's house, but it was Oliver's now.

Technically, this was Julie's home at last, since her father owned it; no longer her aunt's and uncle's, where she had stayed for protracted visits. She'd always had a room here which was hers alone, but now it was a different one—Christine had had one of the grander bedchambers redecorated for her and Julie used it on an occasional weekend. She felt like a guest in it, she'd told me.

143

Frances was still in Antibes, her return delayed by a touch of flu. My parents, too, were still away—in New Zealand at that point. My grandmother had been invited, however. I brought her out with me from town—where she had lived for the past some-odd years, after she had turned the house in Locust Valley over to my mother and father.

"Christine wants to be sure I see how becoming to her the old Thayer mansion is," she remarked as we drove out.

It was with an odd reluctance that I turned in through the gates and headed up the tree-lined drive; not that I wasn't eager to see Julie. Ahead of us loomed the familiar house—like a French chateau, with its Gothic chimneys, steep gray slate roof, and the long, beautiful sixteenth-century Renaissance façade of hand-tooled limestone.

We drew up in front and a parking attendant took away the car.

My throat tightened as we walked into the entrance hall. Above us was the great sweep of marble and bronze staircase, with the stair landing on which sat a grand piano and two sofas, overhung by a twenty-foot tapestry depicting some episode in the life of Charlemagne. The thousands of times I had been here—

And Warren would come no more.

The family were on the terrace at the rear—the long paved terrace with a pierced-stone parapet that ran the whole length of the house. Below it were the formal gardens, surrounding an ornamental pool with a fountain, and beyond that the wide avenue of turf lined on either side with boxwood hedges and adorned at intervals with the statuary Warren's grandfather had long ago bought in France. The lengthy vista ended at the summerhouse.

The central third of the terrace—the part adjoining the main section of the house—had been covered with an awning, making it like an outdoor living room, and spoiling the fine lines of the façade, with its elegant detailing. I couldn't remember anything more extensive than some garden furniture and a table

144

with an umbrella out here before, but now there were settees, and chairs, and tables and lamps.

No guests had yet arrived. There were only Julie, Oliver, and Christine. They made much of my grandmother—as she had expected, I know. My Grandmother Norden is a handsome woman at seventy plus—tall, with a commanding presence, iron-gray hair, and piercing blue eyes. She is kindhearted, but only to those she deems deserving; what she is famous for is saying what she thinks, which can be devastating.

As Christine talked with her, Grandmother kept her eyebrows skeptically lifted a little, and I wondered whether she would let fall one of her pronouncements now, or later on. As they stood together, the older woman of the two made the younger seem, as they say, plastic. Oliver must certainly have married Christine for her looks—a standard blonde prettiness which she still had. But twenty years after the ceremony, anyone meeting her was apt to be impressed most by the maintenance required to achieve her present modish imitation of perfection.

It was a lavish party. Julie warned me, before the deluge of guests, what to expect.

"About two hundred were invited, I think. The tables for dinner are set up in the ballroom, and it's all decorated—you wouldn't know the place. There'll be music, with dancing if anyone can find room. What do you think of the awning, by the way?"

"Your grandfather would have been horrified."

"I know. In his day, if they wanted to be outside, they walked to the summerhouse."

I don't care for large parties. The larger the gathering became, the more I retreated to the sidelines. I was with Julie off and on, and now and then I spotted someone I'd known at school and could exchange a few words with; but most of the guests were middle-aged friends of Julie's parents, with a sprinkling of Richie's friends.

145

I must have had many innocuous conversations with people that night; there must have been long stretches of time when Julie and I were together talking happy, inconsequential talk as any engaged couple would. But the things I remember from the party are the ones that had a bearing on my quandary about Oliver Thayer.

Richie was there. He arrived late. It had turned cool on the terrace by then, and everyone had shifted back into the drawing room, where the waiters carefully made their way, with trays of drink orders, among the groups of people who stood talking in tight little circles.

I was with Julie when her half-brother came up to us and extended his hand to me. "Congratulations, Lex," he said. "I always thought Julie hated your guts, but she tells me I was wrong."

"Thanks, Richie. I'm afraid I thought the same till quite recently."

Richie was a poor and callow imitation of his father. Not as tall, slight in figure, with narrow shoulders. He had the same peculiar indentations as Oliver, on either side of his forehead and in both cheeks, and in his undeveloped-looking face they were a disaster; he gave the appearance of having been ineptly put together again after some horrible accident.

"How's college?" I asked. "You're a sophomore this year?" His grades hadn't been good enough, I knew, to get him into any of the standard colleges—let alone Ivy League. And for some reason he hadn't gone to Downing, where the administration would have had to take him, because of the Thayer endowment of the medical school. The family had had to settle for one of those offbeat experimental schools that had needed money badly enough to admit him.

He shrugged. "Right. I'm back there again. Nothing better to do anyway, I guess. And after I've put in my four years, I'm supposed to go to Harvard Business School. I'm told."

He'd never get into Harvard B-School; I knew that. Some

substitute would have to be found.

"I feel sorry for Richie," Julie said when he'd gone off in search of another drink. "Daddy expects so much of him. The poor kid started to buckle under the load about the time he learned to walk, I guess."

I remembered Stuart Thayer smiling, years ago, over the fact that little Richie was being groomed to challenge Warren when he grew up, for top position. "Why, the child's only six years old!" he'd exclaimed. But Richie had been left a clear field, with Warren disqualifying himself by becoming a fugitive expatriot. And now—

But the picture of Oliver's son heading up the Thayer enterprises simply wouldn't come into focus.

"What kind of trouble was it that Richie was in?" I asked, curious. "You mentioned it to your father at dinner in Montreal, and he almost had a stroke."

"Oh, that." A look of unhappiness crossed her face. "I'm not to talk about it—remember?" She frowned and shook her head. "It was Richie and his friend Mark. I know about it because Richie was frantically trying to locate Daddy and phoned me, hoping I could reach him somewhere. Which I did." She stopped and glanced carefully around, to make sure no one else could hear. We were a little apart from the crowd, standing by a painted panel—a classical French landscape, one of a series that was continued on around the room, each scene set in a gilded stucco design of leaves and flowers.

"I can't tell you all of it. Mark and Richie were at prep school together, and this was their senior year. It was connected with drugs—what happened—and it was much more serious for Mark than for Richie. But bad enough, in any case. Daddy and Mr. Theobald, Mark's father, went up to the school and got it straightened out and hushed up." She pressed her lips together in a thin line. "And don't ever breathe a word about it to anyone. Or mention that boy's name."

It was after that, when Julie'd gone to speak to Christine

about something, that I remember standing with my grandmother, as she watched Oliver being host.

"At last he has it all," she said. "The only fly in his ointment must be that Stuart can't see him enjoying it. For so long he wanted this house—"

"He's wanted everything Stuart ever had, hasn't he?" I added in what must have been a rather savage tone. Mentally including in the list, when it happened to occur to me just then, the double alliance with the Hargreave family. He'd had to settle for the older, plainer sister.

Grandmother's blue-eyed gaze was thoughtful. "You have something against Oliver?" she asked carefully.

"Quite a lot." I'd thought of telling her, on the drive out, of the unsettling conclusion I'd come to about his part in what had happened to Warren. But it had seemed too preposterous to put into words.

"Maybe later you can tell me what the trouble is—but right now you'd better forget it and smile nicely. This is your engagement party, after all." She studied me; turned away to tap her cigarette over an ashtray on the Louis Quinze table nearby. "Not only is Julie joining your family," she said when she looked back at me, "but you are joining hers."

"For better, for worse—"

"Exactly. You don't want to start *off* at odds with your father-in-law. You know, Lex, sometimes I could cut my tongue out. I shouldn't have made that remark about Oliver in the first place. I'm always saying what I like and being sorry afterward!"

"Sorry?" I grinned. "You disillusion me!"

"I'll even retract what I said. Whatever it was. The trouble is I've never liked Oliver particularly. But one must be fair. He's had his cross to bear. He was the son with the business ability, you know, and yet Stuart was made head of everything the family had. Oliver did the work, and his brother got the credit. Can you blame him for wanting things the other way around?

148

Stuart was basically frivolous actually—a glamor boy—"

"I know he was a hell of a nice guy—"

"Oh, yes. Everyone adored Stuart—women, children, and dogs and horses, as the tribute goes. While Oliver's always been attractive enough in his own way, as long as Stuart was around he was overshadowed. What I'm trying to say is there's no reason to condemn him because of—"

"Depends on what you condemn him *for.*"

Julie came up to us then, so that was the end of the conversation.

The party went on. Dinner was announced. The ballroom was decorated beyond the point of recognition—all in pink—with tables set around a small dance floor that had been left in the middle. At one end of the room, between the French windows that gave on the terrace, a seven-piece group played a selection of standards, predictably including *Eleanor Rigby, Yesterday,* and *Blowing in the Wind*—calculated to appease the younger guests without offending the ears of the middle-aged.

I danced with Julie outside on the terrace, and should have been happy. Instead I felt a sense of dread. I was Romeo at the masked ball of my enemy.

The subject of Oliver Thayer was reopened on the way home. Both Grandmother and I were staying for the rest of the weekend at my parents' place, Laurel Hill—the big Georgian house that had been Grandmother and Grandfather Norden's, and in which I'd grown up from the age of six.

"You spoke so *vindictively,* dear, of Oliver—" she began as we neared our house on the short journey, over deserted roads, from the Thayer place. "Why?"

So I told her; told her why, as I now believed, Oliver had sent me to Canada.

By the time I had finished, we were home, and I'd made us each a drink from the bar in the family room.

She sat looking into hers and absently stroking the head of

our big Irish setter, Rusty, which he had rested on her knee. Rusty and the maid were looking after the house while my family were away.

"Do you think Oliver's capable of it?" I asked.

"I think you should forget this whole line of thought of yours. Wipe it from your mind and marry Julie Thayer."

"I can't forget it."

"For Julie's sake you'd better try. That poor child's been a displaced person since she was five years old. She gets on well with Oliver now, and passably with Christine; she doesn't need you causing further dissension."

"I know. But it's because of Julie, among other things, that I can't put this idea—fixation—whatever you want to call it— out of my mind. No matter how much I'd like to. The three of us grew up together—every memory that Julie and I have in common, from childhood to the day we got engaged, has Warren in it. She loved him, too—"

"I'm sure she did. Which is another reason you've got to put aside your suspicions. They're only suspicions, you know— you've no proof. If Julie were to discover what you believe, it would be a disaster. If she doesn't agree with you, you'll lose her. If she decides you're right, you'll have transformed her past, present and future into a nightmare! Do you want that? For her to be forced to believe that her own father could have—"

"Of *course* I don't want that! I didn't want any of this to happen—"

"But it did happen. Warren was killed—we all know *that* at least. The important thing is to let the tragedy stop there."

"And allow Oliver Thayer to get away with it?"

"If he did it. Don't forget the 'if' . . . Lex, an eye for an eye never brought happiness to anyone; nor justice, either. Innocent people suffer, too, when vengeance is done. Try, dear; try to forget this. What is it you have in mind, anyway, a vendetta?"

"I don't *know* what I have in mind."

"I'm not defending Oliver, you see. What happens to him

150

isn't important. It's Julie I care about. And you."

"Yes, I know that, Grandmother."

We finished our drinks; talked a little of my parents. I escorted her to her room, the first one at the top of the circular stair.

"You didn't answer my question," I reminded her. "Do you think he's capable of it?"

"Anyone is capable of anything," she said in annoyance, outdone with me, "given sufficient provocation . . . The real answer to your question is that Oliver Thayer would never do anything he wouldn't want to see written up in the newspapers, if there was a particle of chance that it could become known."

"Which you feel would rule out his arranging for Warren's death?"

"Yes. Putting it that way, I think we've knocked your case against him into a cocked hat. Oliver's a perfectionist, among other things—he wouldn't *allow* anyone to be in a position to expose him for involvement in a crime."

"But the thought of the crime wouldn't stop him—"

"I doubt it. He's quite ruthless."

I agreed.

"Good night, Grandmother."

"Good night, Lex dear." She patted my cheek, smiled sadly at me, and went into her room and closed the door.

Rusty followed me along the wide, familiar hallway and into my room, where he stretched out on the rug by the bed with a sigh of contentment.

How simple things are for him, I thought.

On Monday, Julie called me at work.

"They've found Warren. Up in the mountains near where you were . . . What's left of him, that is."

"Oh." I hadn't known I still cherished any hope, but I had. Its death was quick and painful. Then came the grisly vision conjured up by her words. After that a sense of unreality, coupled with the feeling that actually Warren had been dead a long time—something like ten years.

"Daddy's going up to identify him." She could scarcely talk; her voice was thick with tears. "He'll fly up this afternoon."

"The police don't need me?"

"No. One person will be enough."

"Are you all right?"

"I suppose so. Considering."

She was still at her father's house, she told me. She didn't feel up to driving, but Wallace, the chauffeur, would bring her into town in her car after he returned from taking her father from his office to LaGuardia, where he kept his private plane.

So she was waiting at my apartment when I got home.

Badly in need of something with which to occupy herself, so that she wouldn't have to think, she'd fixed an elaborate veal dish for dinner—prosciutto and cheese sealed up between slices of scallopine. It was probably good, but I don't remember. We were both waiting for the phone to ring. "I told Daddy I'd be here," she'd said when I came in.

We were lying on the big couch beneath the windows, touching, not talking, both of us watching the darkening sky when at last the call came from Montreal.

I'd been more than ever aware, as I lay there, of the watch on my wrist—implacably living a life of its own. I'm not a believer in science fiction, and no watch is more than a collection of parts. This one was self-winding; leave it in a drawer a couple of days and it would stop. But that moment in the Sûreté Headquarters in Montreal when I'd seen it on the counter, its parts in dazzling motion still, when its owner was dead, had had a peculiar emotional effect on me. And now that I wore the thing, it was hardly something I could forget. How many times a day do you look at your watch? And that day, that evening—

The watch undoubtedly influenced my thinking.

The phone rang and I got up to answer it.

"Lex?" It was Oliver.

"Yes."

"It's over. I won't go into details, but there's no doubt that it's Warren. His—well, it's Warren." His voice was smooth, controlled; a measured amount of regret. His tone conveyed the fact that this was, after all, simply the confirmation of a tragedy we all knew had actually occurred two months ago.

I nodded soberly to Julie, sitting with her hands tightly clasped in her lap, that the news was what we'd expected.

"He was under a layer of small stones, with brush piled on top; only five miles from where you parted company with the truck, I understand. Not a dug grave, because Lissing had no shovel."

"No."

"Julie's there?"

"Yes, she is." If my voice sounded odd, he would not be surprised; after all, I'd just had bad news.

"You'll break it to her—"

"Yes. I'll tell her."

"I don't know what the family would have done without you, Lex, through all this—"

"Good night," I croaked, and hung up.

What would *he* have done without me, I thought, was more to the point. Me. And the sharp-faced little man—

"He had no doubt that it was Warren . . ." Julie said.

"That's right. He was sure." My hand still rested on the cradled telephone. A reckless, blinding rage, beginning somewhere in my gut, spread upward until it reached my head. Dots swam before my eyes. I hadn't known anger could be like this —an atavistic force, a thing outside myself that took over and ruled me with a power over which neither will nor reason had any iota of control.

"God damn!" I said thickly. "God damn Oliver Thayer!"

"Lex!" I know she said it, but her voice was far away.

"He used me. He used me to track him down. There was a little weasel-faced man in your father's office the day I first went

153

to see him. He was there when I arrived, and there when I came out, and he tried to hide his face. He's the same man who followed me when I was staying at the Queen Elizabeth, because I saw him clearly, he was in the elevator with me, but he was wearing a wig to look different. He—"

"Lex!" She stared at me in shock. "You can't possibly believe—"

"This man didn't get Warren the day we first met because I'd taken precautions that time. But he followed me from the hotel the night you had dinner with me, and he checked into the Genève fifteen minutes after I got back. He—"

"Lex, you're insane!" She had gotten to her feet, and now she advanced the few steps that brought her right in front of me. "You don't know *any* of this! You're just putting together little pieces of things, haphazard, things that have no connection! You *told* me about the man who wanted a room by the stairs. Daddy knows about him, the police gave him all those details. But there's *no* reason for you to believe—"

"The description matches."

"There are *thousands* of people who match that description. And why would my father—"

"Because to him Warren was a blot on the family escutcheon which he felt must be removed." My head had cleared, the dots no longer danced before my eyes, and I knew that what I was saying to Julie she would find unforgivable. But I had no choice now—the words were out.

"My father," she said, low and very clear, "would not commit murder. Or commission it, either."

"You can't know that for certain." I looked down at her— so close, within my reach, yet hopelessly alienated from me now. "Oh, Julie—I'm sorry!" I started to take her in my arms, but she stepped back.

"Oh, don't be sorry! Have the strength of your convictions!" Her face was stiff, expressionless; onto it she forced the travesty of a smile. "And you mustn't ally yourself now with the family

154

of Oliver Thayer—that would be unthinkable! Murderer; *spawn* of a murderer—"

She turned away. There was nothing I could do, nothing I could say, that would change things back to how they'd been.

"Julie—Julie, don't—"

She picked up her shoulderbag from the chair where she'd left it.

"Whatever happened to the suspect, Ronald Gore?" she asked frigidly as she checked the clasp of her bag.

"I didn't tell you. He did fly to Montreal from New York the day Roy talked with him, and back the same day. No alias— he used his own name. Since there's no record of his crossing the border before that, either by plane or by car, the F.B.I. believe he was in the United States at the time Warren was shot."

"But they can't know that for certain." She parroted back the same statement I'd made to her a minute before.

She stood for a moment framed in the archway to the entrance hall—the cool, poised and unreachable girl I'd known for so many years.

"Good-by, Lex," she said evenly.

11

The day was approaching on which Hugo Praeger would formally announce his candidacy for President of the United States. His fund-raising campaign was going quite successfuly. All over the country, young people had rallied to support him, and according to a just-completed opinion poll a heartening core of middle-aged and older people, disenchanted with the two established parties and their haggling over oil prices and the dilemma of inflation versus recession, indicated that they were ready to follow where Praeger led.

With Julie suddenly removed from my life, and time on my hands that would drive me crazy, I was glad to be able to enlist with Praeger's organization as a worker. I did, and was assigned to spend what time I could at his headquarters, which at present were set up in a couple of rooms in the *Evening Standard* building, where Praeger put out his newspaper.

Sunday, the day after the Thayers' party, *The New York Times* carried the announcement of our engagement, including Julie's picture; Monday Warren's body was identified, and the engagement disintegrated; Tuesday Julie returned to me, by special messenger, the diamond ring I'd bought her at Harry Winston's. Wednesday I went downtown to the *Evening Stan-*

156

dard building, on the Lower West Side, and talked to Praeger. And Thursday when I left my desk at Randell at five o'clock I headed for my new assignment as a political worker.

Friday I took the morning off to go out to Long Island for the small, private burial service for Warren. Neither time nor place had been given in the *Times*, but I'd gotten them from John, Frances's butler.

Frances was back. She pressed my hand as I came up to her in the porch of the church after the short service. "Come and see me," she whispered, and I nodded.

Before I realized that Oliver stood next to her, he had taken my hand. "I'm sorry, Alex. Very sorry." He turned his head slightly in the direction of his daughter, then looked back at me, and I concluded that he was referring not to the departed but to the broken engagement. I passed on without speaking.

"Thank you for coming." It was Christine, who stood next to her husband. The look she gave me was puzzled.

"Julie?" I said tentatively, pausing in front of her. But she did not raise her eyes above the level of my chest. She turned away after a moment and descended the steps to the first of the black limousines that stood in line. One of the mortuary assistants held the door for her and she got in.

It would seem that she hadn't told Oliver of my accusations. If she had, he certainly wouldn't have shaken my hand. None of them knew, I guessed, why she had broken our engagement.

I got into my car and drove back to Manhattan, where people were still congratulating me on my approaching marriage.

My parents came home the next day from Tokyo, and on Sunday I went out to see them. But I didn't stay long—I didn't want my mother prodding me as to what had happened with Julie. They both knew I didn't feel like discussing Warren, either, and sadly they watched me drive away again. Their trip had been a great success; they'd show me the pictures when they got the prints back.

Thursday of the upcoming week—September 18th—was set now for Praeger to announce his candidacy. On Monday I dropped by headquarters after I left Randell, to help out for a while before going home. I was sorting through lists of names when Praeger came in.

"Good evening," I said, looking up.

"How are you, Alex? Good to have you among us. No—sit down." He pulled up a chair to the other side of the table and sat on it. He'd acquired another layer of tan since I'd seen him last week, and I guessed that he'd been out sailing—one of his favorite pastimes—over the weekend.

"I'm not sure whether you've approved—have you," he asked, "of Julie Thayer signing on as one of my staff—"

"Oh." I looked down at the stack of lists before me on the table. "I didn't know that she had. Our engagement happens to be off now."

I looked up in time to see his brows drawn together in a frown. "I'm sorry—" His voice had dropped to a very personal key. "She didn't mention that." He hesitated. "But this job she's taking on may still concern you, perhaps. At her own insistence, she's going to accompany me around town on my daily schedule for the next two or three weeks—or longer, depending."

Oh, *no*, I thought; the idea that I had vetoed.

"She hopes possibly to spot this Ronald Gore whose group are supposedly going to try to take a shot at me. She thinks he and his people are likely to hang about in the vicinity observing my routine."

He must have seen my appalled reaction, because he said, "I know. It sounds as if she might be putting herself in some danger. And I tried to dissuade her." He smiled ruefully. "Unfortunately I can't even claim that all this bravery and devotion on her part is on my account. She tells me it's because of what happened to her cousin, your good friend Warren. She seems to be convinced it was Gore who shot him."

158

"Maybe, maybe not. But she shouldn't be allowed to take such a risk!"

"She's a very determined young lady. And I think the risk is *not* so great. Since your warning I've of course strengthened my security setup. I have bodyguards with me wherever I go. In addition to that, the F.B.I., having had no success so far in tracking down any of this group of Roy Lissing's, are going to supply a detail of undercover agents, as a sort of stakeout, to keep an eye on everything occurring in my vicinity."

Modestly, he shrugged. "As with Julie Thayer, all this is not particularly on my account. It's because the F.B.I. still hope to catch up with Lissing. If they can lay their hands on *any* of this revolutionary group . . ."

"What about the Secret Service? Once you've declared, that is—" Only ten days before, President Ford had looked down the barrel of a revolver pointed at him in Sacramento. There was talk now of extending the protection provided by the Secret Service to the leading presidential aspirants.

"I don't qualify as yet. And not being either a Republican or a Democratic candidate, I'm not sure I ever will. But I'm *well* protected, Lex. So don't worry too much about Julie Thayer."

"When does she start?"

"Tomorrow."

I didn't like it.

I went to see Frances—at a time when I knew Julie would be with Hugo Praeger at a dinner in Washington. On Tuesday.

"Can't you stop her from doing this, Frances?"

"You know I can't, Lex. If Julie were the kind of girl who did what other people wanted her to, I'm sure the two of you would still be engaged."

"Did she tell you what broke it up?"

"No. Though whatever it was, she's not happy over the outcome. Is there anything you can do to mend things?"

159

"Nothing. She'd have to change her mind, and she won't. You saw her at the service Friday—she looked through me as if I weren't there."

"Yes. I'm so sorry. So sorry, Lex."

We talked about Warren, and that didn't cheer either of us any. I didn't want to talk any more about Warren.

Praeger reassured me on Wednesday of that week. I went down to his headquarters after I'd finished my stint at the office, and several of us went over the speech Hugo would make the next day when he announced his candidacy.

He came in from the newsroom, and I couldn't help wondering where Julie was—whether she was somewhere in the building. When he'd chatted with us all a few minutes, he took me aside.

"There's no need to worry about Julie. Her father took a dim view of this job she's doing for me, and he's assigned his car and chaffeur to her till further notice. The chauffeur picks her up at her aunt's apartment every morning, and delivers her back at night. One of my personal guards goes along as well. Just to be sure."

"Thanks for telling me."

Praeger put a hand on my arm. "Probably all a false alarm, anyway. After the massive search that's gone on for these people, they've very likely gone to ground and are lying low."

But they could come out of their holes. Anytime.

The day came, and Hugo Praeger made his announcement during the course of the speech he gave as guest of honor at a luncheon meeting at the Waldorf. He would run for election in 1976.

I was aghast that evening to see Julie's face on TV, very clear and recognizable, in a filmed interview with the announced candidate that had taken place on the sidewalk as he was leaving the hotel. The next morning was even worse—her picture was on the front page of the *Times,* her name given with those of three or four others, including Mrs. Praeger, who'd been standing with Praeger after the luncheon.

Oh, Christ! If Lissing and Gore's bunch hadn't known she was tagging along, with a potentially damning knowledge of some of Warren's friends, they knew it now.

I hardly slept, that Thursday night. Nor Friday. I expected some immediate drastic move against Julie—a sniper in a window, or . . .

The weekend passed uneventfully. I worked most of the day, both Saturday and Sunday, on Praeger for President. We were sorting through a mass of requests for Hugo to speak at places as disparate as Bronxville, New York, and Antlers, Oklahoma, as far apart as Key West and the Yukon.

Monday came. Though I spent part of my day on architecture, things were slack at the office, and my boss was a Praeger fan, so by three I was free to shift to the political backstage. I saw nothing of Praeger that day—he was in at the newspaper offices early, before the *Standard* went to press, and I was there late.

So I saw nothing of Julie either.

That was the day a shot was fired at President Ford—and missed—as he came out of the St. Francis Hotel in San Francisco.

And Hugo Praeger thought the risk was not too great?

When I got back to my apartment a little after nine-thirty, my phone was ringing. I heard it from outside, before I'd gotten the door open, and I knew what it was.

I plunged across the living room, tripping over a chair, and picked up the phone.

"This is John. I've been trying to reach you for Mrs. Thayer—"

161

"What is it?" My heart seemed literally to be in my throat
—I couldn't breath.

"They've taken Miss Julie—"

"Who?"

"Them. We don't know, Mr. Norden." There was a quaver
in his voice. "Two of them."

"I'll be right there, John."

I got a taxi. Traffic was light, but even so the twelve-block
trip seemed to take forever.

There were both uniformed police and plainclothesmen all
over the place. I had to identify myself, and then argue with one
of the uniformed cops, before they would let me in the building.
Same thing before I could be admitted to the Thayer apartment.

John was standing in the foyer, looking like a displaced person. He wasn't even allowed to open the door—a policeman
was doing that; and there were strangers wandering all through
his domain. At the moment, I guessed, he was the family repre-
sentative, as there was no sign of Oliver, or Frances, or for that
matter Christine. John was in charge.

He brightened when he saw me, but as I came to stand beside
him, I saw that his chubby cheeks were waxen, like those of a
corpse, and sweat stood unwiped on his forehead. "Oh, I'm so
glad you've come!" he exclaimed.

"Is there any news of her?"

He shook his head. "No. She's gone—that's all. Gone." His
voice cracked. "Wallace—you know Wallace—" I nodded. Oliver's chauffeur. "Well, he's been bringing her home every evening when she's through working for Mr. Praeger. And one of
Mr. Praeger's personal security men—a bodyguard—comes
with her every time. He sees her to the door of the building,
downstairs.

"But he doesn't come in, you see." His voice cracked a little
again. "There's the doorman, and no one gets past him without
being checked on. You know that, of course—for every visitor,
the doorman rings the apartment owner. If the person isn't

162

okayed by someone living here, he doesn't get in."

"Yes. So what happened?"

"Two people—a man and a girl—came into the building just before Miss Julie came home. They took the doorman by surprise. Held a gun on him. When she arrived, they were standing out of sight. The bodyguard got out of the car with her and came as far as the lobby door. He saw the doorman, Juan, inside, and Juan nodded to him, like everything was all right, and Mr. Praeger's man didn't come in. Just Miss Julie came in. Wallace drove off, and the guard went with him."

"Did they say anything—the two people?"

"Gave orders, that was all. And told Juan not to call for any help for twenty minutes, because they had a man stationed across the street with a rifle. Juan didn't believe that—he called the police as soon as they'd gotten around the corner with her."

"By which time nothing could be done," I said bitterly. "Where had she been this evening?"

"At a dinner at the Americana. With Mr. Praeger."

"Yes, I see." If only she'd never had this reckless idea! If only Hugo Praeger had refused to let her—"I'd better have a word with Mrs. Thayer."

"Yes—she's been expecting you. She's in her room. The doctor's been—to give her something to quiet her nerves."

I talked with Frances for a few minutes in her white and gold bedroom. She lay small and helpless in the canopied bed.

"Has Oliver come yet?"

"I didn't see him as I came in. I'm sure he'll be here."

"John tried to reach him. He had dinner in town, but Irwin didn't know where. Christine's expecting him at the house, so I suppose he's driving out." She stared up at me, her eyes sunken deep in their sockets, the shadows beneath them dark and ugly. "She's all I have. Like my own daughter. You know that, Lex—"

"Yes, I know. Try to sleep, Frances. Everything's being done that *can* be done."

163

Like what? I thought. Everything had been done to try to find Roy and Ronald Gore and their friends for more than two months. And nothing.

Irwin Kuhn had arrived while I was talking with Frances. When I emerged again into the hall, I saw his slight form and neat, shining blond head in the far reaches of the living room, ahead of me. He was talking to someone I took to be a plain-clothesman.

"Hello, Alex," he said as I joined them. "Pretty nasty development, isn't it." He introduced me to Captain Donati of the New York City Police Department—a man with a sallow complexion and a chin like a prize fighter.

"As we were just saying," Kuhn remarked, "the group who abducted her must have known when she was on the way home. They took over downstairs only three or four minutes before she came in."

"They may have had a lookout posted on Madison Avenue," said Captain Donati. "They also must have had someone stationed at the Americana to warn the lookout when she was leaving." That made sense. They couldn't have kept the doorman captive for hours, hoping she'd come in, when there'd be people coming and going—other tenants of the apartment building. The lookout, too—the timing was exactly right; someone on the corner at Madison had only to step into the cross street and signal whoever was waiting at Fifth, a block away, while the car had to go three blocks because of the one-way streets, probably hitting a red light on the way. Taking three or four minutes.

I looked to my left as another man joined us and saw that it was George Cavanaugh, the F.B.I. agent with whom I'd talked before.

"Praeger's right," he said. "She shouldn't have been allowed to help out. Or else we should have given her more protection. We thought of assigning a man to her, but when we learned Praeger had already arranged for one of his private bodyguards to stick with her, it didn't seem necessary."

"Guy didn't do his job properly, either." Captain Donati rocked forward onto the balls of his feet. "He should have taken her up in the elevator and waited till she was locked into the apartment."

"Any of our men would have." Cavanaugh sighed.

At that point Oliver arrived.

I've never seen a man in good, robust health who looked more stricken.

"Any news of her?" He glanced anxiously from the F.B.I. agent to the N.Y.P.D. captain and back.

"Nothing yet, Oliver." It was Irwin Kuhn who answered.

The gaze which swept our group of four was almost accusatory, as though to say that one or all of us must be dilatory in not having more than that to report. "I came as soon as I heard. It was on the car radio—I must have been halfway home—"

Donati filled him in, with Cavanaugh adding some comments. Irwin Kuhn left us, apparently to give instructions to John.

Half of me watched Julie's father—a man who loved the girl I loved; the other half watched Warren's uncle.

Praeger had been to the apartment earlier, I learned—he'd left shortly before I had arrived.

Wallace, the chauffeur, had been questioned, the slipshod bodyguard had been questioned.

Juan, the doorman, had told everything he could remember.

"The man may have been Ronald Gore," Captain Donati said. "Right physical type, and when they showed the doorman a series of police-artist sketches, he picked the one that Julie Thayer had helped on, the one of Gore. I got word of that identification only a few minutes ago."

"And the girl?" I asked.

"About five-feet-eight, brown hair—long, almost to her waist. The doorman didn't notice anything else—said she was behind him most of the time."

165

Donati turned to Cavanaugh. "Till Miss Thayer joined Praeger as an eagle-eye scout, I imagine this group—whatever they call themselves—couldn't have been aware that their plans for an assassination attempt were known."

"Probably not. They might have guessed that Warren Thayer talked, but they didn't know."

"So now they're warned."

"And so are we." George Cavanaugh, I thought, was like the personification of the ideal insurance salesman—friendly, helpful; so average-looking you'd never pick him out in a crowd. "Since they've gone to the trouble and risk of removing Julie Thayer from the scene of action, we can be sure they're determined to carry out their purpose—the assassination of Hugo Praeger. We'll be ready for them."

Oliver glared at him. "But I don't give a damn about Praeger! What are you doing to get my daughter back?"

"Everything possible! There are a lot of men working on this, Mr. Thayer—"

"We're assuming they'll hold her for ransom," the captain said. "She's certainly worth money to them." He looked levelly at the head of the Thayer family and all its enterprises. "Quite a good deal, I imagine."

"We're treating it as a routine kidnap case, Mr. Thayer," George Cavanaugh agreed. "As far as the media are concerned —or the people who have taken her, for that matter. There will be no mention of an assassination plot, only the assumption that she's being held for ransom. In fact right now, if you'll draw up a statement for the reporters we've got on hand, to the effect that money will be paid immediately, and all demands and conditions met—"

John was at his elbow. "Mrs. Thayer is asking for you—"

"Yes, in a minute. Get me pen and paper, will you, John?"

He worked over a statement, with Cavanaugh advising him, and then went off to see Frances.

He was gone for a little while, and I wandered around the

166

living room and into the library and out again into the foyer, hoping there would be some word of progress.

Oliver came along the hall and stopped beside me. "I heard it on the car radio." He'd already said so, when he'd first arrived. He probably didn't remember that I'd been standing with him then. "I just couldn't believe it! I have Julie's car, you know, since I insisted she use mine, with Wallace. Safer for her, I thought.

"John and Irwin tried to reach me after it happened. Irwin thought I'd gone to my club for dinner. That's what I'd told him, but I changed my mind and went to Lutèce. I was halfway home, I suppose, when I heard.

"And Hugo Praeger!" His penetrating eyes glinted in anger. "That this should happen to my daughter because of him! They can shoot him down in the street anytime, as far as I'm concerned, and the world would be better off! Damned radical!"

Cavanaugh came up to Oliver. "Where will you be tonight, Mr. Thayer—here?"

"At the Pierre. It's where I stay when I'm in town." He'd maintained a suite there for years, I knew.

"The Pierre. All right—" The F.B.I. agent started to turn away, but changed his mind as he thought of something. "Oh. I meant to ask you, Mr. Thayer. When you went to Canada to identify your nephew's body, did they tell you the cause of death?"

Oliver seemed nonplused. "Well, I assumed the bullet wound—"

Cavanaugh shook his head. "They didn't tell you, then—"

"All I was informed of was where he'd been found. The medical examiner—or whoever—hadn't yet looked at the—remains."

"His report has just reached me. The base of the skull was bashed in. It's assumed your nephew died of the blow. Or blows."

I stared at the man, that whole hideous trip in the panel truck

167

back in my mind again.

"His *skull* was bashed in?" Oliver Thayer looked stunned.

"Easy," I grated, "to finish off someone who's half in a coma."

"Yes. Roy Lissing," said George Cavanaugh, "apparently couldn't wait."

As John let me out of the apartment, I had a final glimpse, over one shoulder, of Oliver looking drained and ill, like a man who's had one blow too many.

I fought off the press, when I reached the street; beat a retreat between two parked cars. One of them was Julie's Porsche— I recognized it sitting in the no-parking zone.

I got loose eventually, though I ran more than a block to shake the most persistent of my pursuers. And headed desolately home.

12

I settled on the long living-room couch with the radio. I wished that I smoked, because it would have given me something to do. I tried TV, but it only irritated me. I made myself a drink, and then another, but neither did anything to dull anxiety. I turned to coffee.

I'd have gone out for a walk, but I was afraid the phone might ring in my absence. So I wandered from room to room, keeping my ears tuned for any news-break in the music. Eventually I had three radios on—one in the living room, one in the bedroom, and the portable in the kitchen. I didn't want to miss a syllable if there was any new development.

Every half hour the news was given. Each time, it stopped me in my tracks, held me motionless, hardly breathing, till the part about Julie was over—and then I continued my wandering. The few sentences about the kidnapping were always the same: no change in the situation. Once in a while I sat down, once I pounded the arms of my favorite chair till the dust flew out of the upholstery; but moving about seemed the least agonizing way of helping the time pass. I needed something to do.

Coming into the bedroom for the fiftieth time or so, I stood bemused. I'd never liked the room—it was too small. It gave

169

me claustrophobia. For some reason just at that moment the thought of Warren's single-room apartment in Montreal came to me, and the marvelous thing Eve had made of it. I felt a surge of interest. What could be done with these four white walls? I could do something now instead of going slowly out of my mind.

My eye lit on the framed color photograph of the city of Florence that hung on the wall opposite the bed.

Yes. Florence was one of my favorite places. I rushed off to my study for my drawing pencils. Came back and tested them on the flat off-white paint. The surface took the pencil very well; it smudged a little if I tried, but that was all right—perhaps when I'd finished I could spray the wall with some sort of fixative.

I began. Once I'd worked out the proportions I wanted, and blocked out the scene, the work was fairly mindless—mechanical, precise drawing. I concentrated on it with all the energy of sublimated worry, and drew with a speed I'd never been capable of in my professional efforts.

The project was a godsend.

A lot of energy must go into worry, because by six o'clock my view of Florence was completed on the wall. Nothing like Eve's romantic and humorous art; my mural was an architect's drawing of the buildings—exact, all done in lines, with no fuzziness anywhere. The Duomo dominated the wall, the famous dome by Brunelleschi quite unmistakable.

The effect of the pencil on the white paint was exactly right —not sharp and black, but soft and shaded—giving the scene some of the grayness that to me is the look of Florence.

All night I'd had the scheduled news, and the bulletins. If there were any new developments, they hadn't been given out to the media. No further bad news; no good news either.

At six-thirty I showered and then had breakfast. Watched the *Today Show* when it came on. There was an interview with Juan, the doorman, and a shot of Oliver avoiding reporters. I didn't learn anything I hadn't already known.

I was just turning off the TV set when my phone rang. I rushed to answer it.

"Lex?" It was my father. "We've just heard the news, your mother and I—"

I told him there was nothing they could do.

I called John. Warren's mother was as well as could be expected, and still under sedatives. It would be best if I hung up, because the police, who were there, were hoping a call might come in from the kidnappers, with a ransom demand.

I hung up.

On the bottom half of the front page of my morning *Times* there was a picture of my ex-fiancée which I could hardly bear to look at. I scanned the paper, but I couldn't have told anyone, afterward, what the news was that day aside from what was on the front page, and that seemed all of a piece—Julie kidnapped, Ford shot at, and there was even a news item on Lee Harvey Oswald: "F.B.I. Focus of Inquiry on Oswald Note," the headline ran. Times didn't change; only the people involved.

It must have been a little before eight-thirty that the phone rang again, and I leaped to answer it.

"Mr. Norden—this is Kevin Stein of the *Daily*—"

"I'm sorry, I know nothing about the case that hasn't already been in the news. I have nothing to say."

Only the first call of possibly many, I imagined.

When the time came at which I should have been at my desk at work, I called my boss and told him I wouldn't be in.

"Sure, Lex," Sam answered. "You know we're not so busy you can't be spared for a few days. I'm sorry—saw the paper this morning, of course."

"Yeh, thanks, Sam."

Another reporter called. Then my grandmother called . . .

I went over to Frances's apartment at about ten o'clock. Oliver was there. Strangely, my animosity toward him seemed to have evaporated—at least for the moment. Whether or not he had plotted to have his nephew murdered seemed a pointless consideration when the most important thing in the world to both of us that day was the same: the life of his daughter.

He was in better shape than he'd been the night before. I think he'd gotten some sleep. And he was too strong a character not to be able to adjust to whatever blows might befall him. Though there was a haunted look still about his eyes.

There were two detectives in the apartment, waiting for the hoped-for call about ransom.

"The F.B.I. is working in conjunction with the city police," Oliver explained, "but technically it's not a federal case—so far. There's no reason to suppose she's been taken across the New York State line. After twenty-four hours, I understand, they can assume that she may have been."

"But the F.B.I. are looking for Gore—"

"They are indeed. Though oddly—to be technical again— only as a lead to Lissing. It's Lissing who's on their 'wanted' list."

Whatever the technicalities, however, they were all working on the case.

Frances was up—a fuzzy sort of zombie because of the sedatives or tranquilizers or whatever the doctor had prescribed. She looked not only ravaged, but odd—she had had trouble drawing on her eyebrows, and one of them canted off at a strange angle, giving her a quirky expression.

The three of us sat in the library, out of the way of the police. Frances was positioned in front of the ebony and mother-of-pearl chess table, where she had laid out a game of solitaire, but I don't think she even saw the faces of the cards. She kept going through the pack, but never played one card upon another.

Seeing them together—Julie's father and her aunt—bleakly discussing possibilities, I wondered, for the first time, whether their relationship had had a bearing on Warren's fate. Frances had refused Oliver Thayer long ago, and married his brother.

172

Though none of it mattered any more, it seemed to me that morning.

Only Julie mattered.

I left a phone number with John—the one for Praeger's headquarters. And then I went down to the Lower West Side to help on more lists of people for Praeger. In my current condition, such work as this was within my scope, whereas I couldn't have gone to Randell and undertaken anything; working with the thought and precision required for an assignment in the office was not at all the same, either, as the manic execution of a mural on one's wall while in the grip of a compulsion.

I had brought my portable transistor radio from home, and I settled to work with it tuned in, at my elbow.

Praeger came in soon after, and made a beeline for the corner where I was working. He placed both hands on the table and leaned on them, stiff-armed, looking down at me. His face was drawn. "I'm sorry. I'm so damned sorry!"

"Yes, I know." It didn't even occur to me to get to my feet, as it ordinarily would have; and this was the potential President of the United States. I wasn't reacting any more, I was simply existing, bleary-eyed with exhaustion and discouragement.

"This thing's entirely my fault. I had no right to let her—"

"You couldn't have stopped her. You said so yourself."

His lips were cynical, his voice corrosive. "But naturally I could have. I'm running my own campaign, I'm the boss of all that goes on in my division of this political game. Do you think I couldn't have turned her down? And now—

"I suppose I didn't actually take seriously the threat these people pose. I paid enough attention to the warning to beef up my security—after Bobby Kennedy and George Wallace, I'd be crazy not to have. And then these *two* attempts against Jerry Ford. But I have not actually *believed* that eventually someone is going to point a gun at me and squeeze the trigger."

173

It is hard—I knew that—to believe hypothetically in one's own death . . .

He straightened up, and belatedly I got to my feet.

"Yesterday," he said caustically. "Last night, that is, after the news that someone had taken that shot at the President, I told Julie her job was off. She wasn't to come with me today, or any more . . . But I decided that too late.

"I can only hope they'll let her go. When they've had their shot at me."

I could see bitter self-condemnation in his eyes—that once again reminded me of my late friend Warren's.

I was standing at the window a little later when Hugo Praeger left the building. We were on the second floor, with windows looking over the street—a rather dingy street, it was, with warehouses, and some run-down offices and stores. I saw Praeger come out, and I watched, curious to see his security force in action. Two cars stood at the curb. He and two husky companions got into the first of them, and the pair of vehicles moved off together. Another car about seventy feet behind on the one-way street swung out from its parking slot and trailed after them; whether that was coincidence or the car in fact contained F.B.I. agents, I didn't know.

It was raining. Raining hard.

At lunchtime a co-worker brought me a pastrami on rye from a delicatessen a few blocks away near the Independent Subway station. I munched it and drank my Coke while I looked over a copy of today's *Evening Standard,* fresh from the presses in the basement and smelling of new ink. A glimmer of optimism had crept into the reports of the Thayer kidnapping, but it didn't sound as if it were based on anything more relevant to the case than the inevitable tendency of the police to hint at eventual success even when they hadn't a single lead. Or *especially* when, I brooded, they hadn't a single lead.

At five the radio was still optimistic, but I was not. I was also dead tired.

174

I wanted to be home in time to watch the six o'clock news, so I left, and after picking up some potato salad and roast beef and a piece of cheesecake at the delicatessen, took the E train —about the only way to get efficiently from the Lower West Side to anywhere on the Upper East Side, especially during rush hour. Then I walked uptown from Fifty-third Street, and when I reached my apartment building had to fend off two reporters who were waiting on the sidewalk.

There was a note from my mother propped on the TV in the living room. She'd come with my father when he'd driven in to his office. Was sorry to have missed me. Had tried Randell, but of course I wasn't there.

Well, it was kind of her, but I don't know what the two of us would have done all day, just sitting knee to knee. It was the thought that counted—the visit wouldn't have cheered me up.

The six o'clock news was a rehash of old stuff. It also flipped through a montage of vintage news shots, beginning with one of Julie as a child of three with her mother; Julie winning a blue ribbon with one of her jumpers; Julie as a debutante; crewing for her cousin Warren; skiing at Aspen; posing with her father at a party in Monaco; in Montreal, flanked by Oliver and me as we came out of the Regency Hotel; with me, coming out of "21," where we'd had lunch together way back early in August. The other recent family tragedy—and the notoriety of her cousin which had preceded it—was touched on, and naturally her engagement to me—with the rumor appended that the engagement was, in fact, off.

All guaranteed to twist the knife in the wound.

After my brief and joyless supper I went to see Frances again. The visit didn't net me anything. She was asleep, Oliver wasn't there, and neither John nor the waiting detectives had anything to contribute other than speculation—and considerable pessimism because there'd been no word from the kidnappers.

But then they weren't holding her for ransom, I thought; that wasn't the reason. They mightn't be holding her at all—

175

"You'll let me know if *anything* happens," I said to John.

Nothing happened. I went home and fell asleep on the couch while waiting for the ten o'clock news on television.

Wednesday. I woke in one of the small hours of the morning, still on the couch in a living room lit only by the colored flicker of the TV—senseless with its sound turned to inaudible.

Shock and despair hit me all over again; and in those dark pre-dawn hours even a glimmer of hope, when you need it most, can be impossible to find.

I switched on a couple of lights and dragged myself into the bathroom, where I rinsed my face with cold water.

There's something terribly cheerless about lights newly turned on at such an hour—a connotation of things gone wrong; alarm; disaster impending. I turned them off.

I got undressed and went to bed, but I lay there sleepless, aching with the memory of the times I'd shared this room with Julie.

I gave up at about five-thirty, and went out to the kitchen for some breakfast. I was ravenous, I discovered when I started cooking. I fixed half a package of bacon and four eggs, and finished the cheesecake.

The kitchen radio was still on from the night before. I wasn't expecting any news—if there'd been any, someone would have called me. But I listened anyway.

Rehash again; with a note of apprehension on account of the failure of Julie Thayer's abductors to make contact—

I went out and got my *Times*. There were a few well-chosen words from Oliver: the family were hopeful, they were waiting for the ransom demand, they would obey to the letter any instructions from the kidnappers, he personally had every expectation that—etcetera.

I went all through the newspaper, from front to back. Hoping beyond all reason, I suppose, to find in some obscure item a clue that could lead to one of the members of Warren's group, or to the place where Julie was being held.

What I found hadn't to do with Julie. It was an obituary of one Philip J. Theobald. It wasn't only the name Theobald that caught my attention, bringing with it the memory of Oliver Thayer's sudden anger, at dinner in Montreal, and an echo of my conversation with Julie, about Richie, the night of the party I didn't want any more to remember; it was the face in the *Times* photograph that riveted my eyes to the page.

Theobald was the man who had waited in Oliver's office; the man who had stood behind me in the elevator in Montreal.

And—I didn't doubt—who had taken the room by the stairs at the Hôtel Genève.

Mr. Theobald had died on Monday night as the result of injuries sustained when he had been robbed.

There were two reasons, it seemed, for his rating a picture on the *Times* obit page: one, he had formerly been a fund-raising specialist of considerable repute and had numbered among his clients several well-known colleges and universities (my eye lit at once on Downing University, of which the Thayer School of Medicine was a part); and two, he had for the last fifteen years or more been a free-lance writer of solid reputation. He'd written four books on financial subjects, all how-to treatments for the layman, and had produced a tremendous number of articles on both finance and sports. Fishing, hunting, horses had frequently been his subjects.

Hunting?

I searched through Tuesday's paper and found the small item about the slaying. Theobald had been discovered in the driveway of his home in Scarsdale, lying next to his car with his head beaten in. His wallet, containing no cash, had been tossed into the shrubbery. So far, the motive for the killing was presumed to have been robbery.

I sat back in my easy chair and stared across the room at the early morning light in the sky outside my windows. I was thinking about what Eve had said—something about the un-

177

likelihood of anyone's ever connecting an inconspicuous murder, or possibly a supposed accident, with a socialite millionaire.

Monday night Oliver had been en route from a restaurant on East Fiftieth Street to his home on Long Island. Presumably via the Midtown Tunnel or the Queensboro Bridge. But it is *possible* to reach Scarsdale from Fiftieth Street via the East River Drive, the Triborough Bridge, Bruckner Expressway and the Hutchinson River Parkway in under half an hour (driving in nighttime traffic), and to reach Long Island afterward from Scarsdale by means of the Whitestone Bridge, without any strain. Not a route one would pick except for a very good reason —but feasible if necessary.

And on Monday night Oliver Thayer, having lent his chauffeur to his daughter, had been quite alone in the car he drove.

13

I squirreled the items about Theobald away in a drawer. That day the only thing I could really concern myself about was Julie.

I felt a great urge to *do* something about her situation. What occurred to me was to try sticking close to Praeger, as she had done. Roy Lissing might be somewhere on hand—and I knew what he looked like. He was wanted for sure in Canada; Quebec or Ontario versus New York State probably didn't make much difference either way. He might well have slipped across the border to help Ronald Gore on their big project.

Praeger would be at the newspaper offices—by now it was after eight. He was always there early, checking the paper as it went to press.

I took the subway. Emerged from its dank passages that smelled of chewing gum, spittle, urine and old puddles, and at the top of the crowded, littered stairs turned toward the Hudson. It was raining, as it had been yesterday and would be again tomorrow, on account of Hurricane Eloise, down in the Gulf region.

I'd had sense enough to put on my raincoat, but I wore no hat. It was pouring—really pouring; rain pelted into my face and ran down from my sopping hair.

I was about three blocks from the *Evening Standard* building, and was blinking the water out of my eyes, when I saw her. Eve—standing in the partial shelter of a doorway recessed between two store windows fifty feet ahead, near the intersection. Even in the murk and rain there was no mistaking the appealing, provocative face, the strange, childish dark eyes under the black rain hat. She was looking toward me, but immediately she glanced away again in the other direction, so I knew she hadn't picked me out of the crowd.

She appeared to be waiting for someone.

I strode ahead with my heart pounding. I must reach her before she recognized me and bolted; but if I made a dash for her, I'd only draw premature attention to myself.

She was alone, apparently. Yes—waiting. For something, or someone.

And then, just before I reached her, she turned and spoke to a person I could not see in the doorway behind her.

"Eve!" I said, grabbing her wrist. At the same instant my gaze passed over her head and met that of a man who stood in the doorway.

Overage cherub, Julie had said. Yes—but not with his curly blond locks gone. He'd shaved his head. The cherub cheeks, the curvy lips, he still had, and they were doubly ugly with the shiny, incredibly round pate. He had a head like a pumpkin. The dead eyes were staring into mine—not in alarm, or even in surprise, but as though I were something he was going to trample on in a minute.

"Lex!" Eve cried out.

Already I was moving to grab Gore and to block him in the corner of the doorway so that he couldn't escape. I stepped to the left, past Eve. I was several inches taller than Gore, and broader in the shoulders; I should have no trouble holding onto him.

180

But I am also completely inexperienced in hand-to-hand combat.

He hit me in the stomach with his right and followed with a left to the jaw. At the same moment that the second blow landed, Eve, whose wrist I still held, tried to jerk away. The two things combined almost caused me to lose my balance, and I stepped backward toward the street to save myself. In a split second, Ronald Gore dodged past me and away around the corner.

The wind was half knocked out of me from the blow to my stomach, but I plunged after him, recovering my breath as I went and dragging Eve with me.

We rounded the corner, and I could see Gore ahead of us, running uptown, threading his way through the damp crowds on the sidewalk.

It is much harder for two people linked together, than for one, to make rapid progress through a swarm of humanity moving at a slower rate. Especially when one of the two is dragging her feet and trying to get loose.

When the pedestrian traffic became too thick, Gore dodged out into the street, and so we did the same.

Eve was clawing at the back of my right hand with her fingernails. She also pleaded with me to stop. "I can't run any more," she panted. "Stop! Please stop!"

And we weren't gaining on him; we were losing. Yet nothing in this world would have made me relinquish my hold on Eve. A bird in the hand is worth more—

I wove our way across streets even with moving cars in them, suicidally dashing in front of speeding taxis, bluffing truck drivers who had to slam on their brakes.

If only there were a police car, or a cop on a corner along here—

No luck. All the police in New York were somewhere else.

A taxi wouldn't help me either—this was a one-way street,

southbound. That was the reason he'd gone north, no doubt.

I was losing sight of him now. Desperately I clamped an arm around Eve's waist, holding tight to her wrist on the far side, and practically carried her.

We made a little faster progress than before, past people huddling under their umbrellas, but just as I'd become encouraged, we were hopelessly stopped at a traffic light. I'd been lucky till now with the traffic signals, but this time we were truly stopped until it changed.

I peered over heads in the next block, and still spotted the ugly round one. Much too far away.

"You'll never catch him!" Eve gasped.

The light changed to green and I hurried across with my unwilling companion. I couldn't see Gore. But I dragged the two of us along the block. At the next corner I glanced up the cross street. Its sidewalks were almost empty of people; there were a couple of trucks being unloaded, but not much other activity. At the far end of the block Ronald Gore, unimpeded by other pedestrians, trotted along.

I broke into a run. I thought at that point of abandoning Eve, on the premise that I'd be able to overtake the man ahead of me. But he, too, having glanced over his shoulder and seen me, started running.

He was too near the intersection with the next street for me to catch him before he got there. And so I still hung onto Eve.

He turned the corner, going downtown—out of sight. I put on a burst of speed, in a panic for fear he would simply have disappeared by the time I reached the intersection. With superhuman effort, it seemed, I came abreast of the brick building around which Gore had vanished; passed it and swung in a right-angle turn around the corner.

There he was, a block away. With his hand on the door of a taxi. As I watched, the traffic light for which the cab had been stopped changed to green. Ronald Gore stepped in and closed the door, and the car took off like a greyhound at the track.

182

I didn't say anything. I couldn't. For a moment the face of the man who'd gotten away was framed in the rear window of the taxi—blurred by the water on the glass, but still wearing, unmistakably, a grin of triumph.

I turned to Eve. "Is she all right?" My breath rasped in my throat, and my tongue was so dry it stuck to the roof of my mouth.

She didn't answer. Too out of breath, maybe. But I was afraid she'd decided not to talk at all.

Well, I'd shake something out of her.

I grasped her now by both wrists. "Eve—I know your group is holding Julie Thayer. Help me get her free . . . and I'll let you go."

The dark eyes under the straight brows regarded me narrowly. "So have me arrested, if you want. The pigs can't charge me with anything—I haven't killed anybody, or blown up anything, or robbed any banks—"

"You're involved in a kidnap plot."

"No."

I gritted my teeth. "But I *know* you are!"

Quickly she shook her head. "All I know about what's happened to Julie is what I've read in the paper."

"But she *is* being held by your friends—"

No answer. She looked away and sighed in apparent boredom. Water dripped from her hat brim and ran in streams down her silky black raincoat.

What could I do with her? I wondered. If I turned her over to the police, they could question her, certainly, but they'd get nothing out of her. The chances were better that I could get through to her myself. Because of Warren.

We were standing in the middle of the sidewalk, a snag in the stream of pedestrians. "Come over here—out of the way." Holding her still by one wrist, I propelled her back to the comparative quiet of the cross street up which we had so recently pelted. We took refuge in a doorway—though the rain,

183

I noticed, seemed to be letting up.

"We'll start over," I suggested. I looked down at the slight, sandy-haired girl who had loved Warren and had fought for his life, and I found that I couldn't think of her as the enemy. "Whose side are you on—theirs or Warren's?"

The question startled her. "What do you mean?"

"I think you know. Warren was against killing Hugo Praeger. He and Roy disagreed; he and *Ronald* disagreed."

"I didn't know we were talking about Praeger. And you think there's a plot to *kill* Mr. Praeger? It's nothing I've heard of."

"Look, Eve—" I tried not to sound exasperated. "You're not in court; and I'm not recording what you say on a tape recorder. This is just you and me talking. Warren told me about the plot."

She hesitated. "Okay, so he told you. But he wouldn't have gone against the others; we all stick together. He argued—sure. But eventually he would have come around."

"He didn't. That's how he got himself killed. The reason he came to see me that morning at the Hôtel Genève was to give me a warning for Praeger."

"Oh, man, what an approach!" Her eyes raked me. "You're trying to tell me Warren died attempting to save Praeger's life? And so I should join *your* side? *Uncle Oliver* had Warren killed! It had nothing to do with Praeger—*or* our friends!"

"I haven't finished," I said. "And I'm not talking now about who killed him, but about *why* he was there that morning—why he was there to get shot at. I'm telling you he came to inform on your group because he was for Praeger—"

Suddenly she drew in her breath in a little gasp. "Warren's watch!" Her eyes were fixed on my left wrist, where the watch showed below the sleeve of my raincoat; she had been on my other side during the blocks we'd chased Gore, and it had been the right hand whose skin she shredded with her nails.

She reached out and touched with a finger what had been

184

Warren's, with a sort of tenderness. "He knew he was dying and he gave it to you?"

"No." I spoke slowly, with chill precision. "It was hocked in Toronto the day after you last saw him. By a man answering the description of Roy Lissing."

She looked up at me. "Roy didn't tell me that . . . I suppose he needed the money badly enough; of course he did. But to *hock* it—" There was a glitter of tears in her eyes.

"Eve—" I put a hand on her shoulder. "I told you I hadn't finished . . . You remember the pink tetracycline capsules Roy got for Warren?"

"Of course."

"The bottle was labeled tetracycline, but when the capsules were analyzed, they were found to be only gelatin."

"Gelatin?" She frowned up at me. "I don't believe you."

"If they'd been a prescription item, the capsules would have been printed—each one of them—with a distinguishing mark. So that any pharmacist could tell at a glance what they contained. These were plain—no markings. It was Julie who noticed. I still had the bottle you'd given me when we left the farm."

She was staring straight in front of her. "I know there were no markings—" she said tentatively. "I remember quite clearly . . . I remember everything that happened—every single thing—"

I still held her by the wrist, below the cuff of her coat. Unconsciously she was rubbing the fingers of that hand with the other—I suppose because I was holding too tight.

"What are you getting at?" She looked up at me. "You believe Roy deliberately gave Warren some nothing capsules instead of an antibiotic?"

"I don't see any other explanation."

"You're sure about the capsules . . . ?"

"Quite sure. They were analyzed at the Sûreté du Québec lab in Montreal."

"He and Warren disagreed, but . . . To let him suffer, let him die inch by inch with the wrong medicine—" She put her hand to her mouth, and bit on the knuckle of her forefinger.

"Nor is that quite all. Lissing ran out of time, and then he killed him."

She took her finger out of her mouth. Without seeing them, her eyes followed the cars splashing by in the busy street beyond us, where for the time being the rain had stopped. "He died of the infection . . ." But she didn't sound too sure. "Roy said he died on the way to the hospital."

"Roy took us the opposite direction from any hospital. Up in the mountains. And Warren didn't have *time* to die of the infection. He died because his head was bashed in."

She turned away and gave a dry sob. "Oh, God!"

"I'm sorry, Eve." Awkwardly, I waited. "You know, I've thought of you often since that day. I've wanted to tell you how sorry I've been on your account, about Warren."

But she had recovered quickly. "Oh, sure! You're only sucking up so I'll tell you about Julie Thayer." From tender she'd switched straight back to tough.

"That's not so." I was angry. "Can't you tell sincere from fake? I'm hardly a crafty sort, Eve. And I don't say things I don't mean. Certainly I hope you'll tell me where Julie is, but not because I've gotten *round* you; because I've gotten *through* to you. Because of Warren, damn it!"

She was quiet. Thinking. "What are you planning to do with me?" she asked, lifting her imprisoned hand, and mine with it.

"Any reason I shouldn't turn you over to the police?" I was only putting pressure on her, really; I'm not sure I could have brought myself to the point of handing Warren's girl over to the authorities. Some vestigial form of schoolboy's honor, I suppose —reluctance to betray a member of one's peer group to those in charge.

"Let me go," she said evenly, "and I'll tell you where to find Roy."

186

A slight thrill of excitement changed the rhythm of my breathing. "Is Julie where Roy is?"

"No. That's why I can give you Roy. As a gift—and may he rot in hell!"

"No deal. I've got to get Julie Thayer safely back. And I don't care how I do it."

"I can't help you."

"I'm sure you can." I was thinking now in terms of holding my captive as a hostage; working on her, wearing her down. Though how—

"They'll let her go," Eve said. "When they're ready."

"Just like they took Warren to a hospital."

She shook her head in denial.

Abruptly a police siren rose to full cry, fairly near at hand, and Eve started violently.

I pulled her with me back to the sidewalk of the main street in time to see the patrol car speed by, its red roof lights flashing. Another police car was hard on its tail.

People around us, craning their necks in only faint interest, brushed against us and then continued on their way. Farther downtown I could hear more sirens—though I had no time then to wonder about them.

"We'll get a taxi," I said coldly to Eve. "The driver will know where the precinct house is." I stepped to the curb to flag down a cab.

"I won't tell them anything," she said fiercely. "Nothing! Not even where Roy is. Don't you want to know that?"

I hesitated. I did indeed want to know where Roy was—and he might—it was possible—lead the police to the others, including Gore.

"Roy's in Ottawa. At seventeen-twenty-three Wapawnet Street." She put her free hand on my arm to hold my attention while she spelled Wapawnet, to be sure I got it.

"Okay."

"Now let me go."

I would have done anything rather than let her go; she was my link with Julie. Had I *said* I'd let her go? But with no warning she jerked loose. My hand and her wrist were wet with sweat from the heat of contact, and with a single twist she slipped free and ran, screaming, as she looked fearfully back at me over her shoulder.

Since I automatically took off after her, the attention of passers-by focused on me immediately. For all you hear about the number of New Yorkers who turn blind and deaf in the proximity of a crime being committed, there are on the contrary plenty of Good Samaritans.

One of these stepped from the side of the truck he was unloading and put himself squarely in front of me. "Hold it, mister!" he said. I attempted to shove him aside, but someone else grabbed me from behind, and I turned to find myself cheek to cheek with a very large black man. I tried to break his grip, but he had a hammer lock on me.

Become involved in a scuffle on the sidewalk, of course, and you are sure to attract the police. They arrived and I was handed over to them—two officers in a patrol car. By which time Eve was irretrievably lost in the throng of people that every day jams the sidewalks of Manhattan.

In the middle of trying to convey to the two patrolmen my urgent need to get in touch with the F.B.I., I learned what all the sirens had been on account of.

Someone had shot Hugo Praeger.

14

The rest of that day I waited. Once the F.B.I. had Roy Lissing's address in Ottawa, and the New York police had my description of Ronald Gore, I was relegated to the sidelines, and whatever news I got was no fresher than the rest of the public's.

Praeger hadn't been killed. There were two bullets in him, and he'd been rushed to a hospital for surgery. The shots had come from the window of a loft quite a way up the street and across, with a good view of the doorway to the *Evening Standard* building. The loft, which was vacant, had been broken into, and evidence on the premises indicated that whoever had shot Hugo Praeger had been waiting and watching for some time. The telescope-sighted rifle and two ejected shells had been found there, but the person who'd fired them had been gone when police reached the place.

The dark side of this news for me—in addition to the unhappy fact of Hugo Praeger's having been gunned down—was the question of what would happen to Julie now. The group's mission was not accomplished, so unless their target died of his injuries, they were unlikely to release their captive. But to continue to keep her (if she was alive) in prolonged imprison-

189

ment was dangerous to the entire group back of this assassination attempt.

The chances were large, now, that they'd simply kill her.

I holed up in my apartment with the TV and my radios. Set to work on another wall of the bedroom, this time blocking out the Ponte Vecchio, with its shops that span the Arno—using for guidance an album of my own photographs of Florence.

Sometime after I got home I discovered, to my amazement, that I was no longer the possessor of Warren's wristwatch. I smiled—for probably the only time that day. Anyhow Eve wouldn't hock it.

I was quite content, actually, to get my Accutron out of a drawer and put it back on.

There were bulletins from time to time on Praeger. One bullet in the neck and one in the arm. It was the first of those that sounded bad—he could end up paralyzed like George Wallace.

Damn Ronald Gore!

And what was he planning to do with Julie?

The only thing I could build any hope on was the possible capture of Roy Lissing. Not that I imagined he would talk; but some lead might be turned up in the place where he was staying, or on him, that would point the way to Ronald Gore. And Julie?

I worked all afternoon—till my father turned up on my doorstep at a little after five.

"I thought we could have dinner together," he said.

He looked fit, as always, I saw as he came on into the apartment, but I noticed he was beginning to seem more definitely middle-aged. His light hair was thinning perceptibly across the top and his mild, square face was getting jowly.

I was glad to see him. I felt as if I'd been alone against the rest of the world for a long, long time.

We went down to the Harvard Club, in the continuing rain. It seemed a reassuring place to go—the dark, cavernous lounge with its leather chairs is as comfortable as the womb, and the great, high-ceilinged dining room, with the paneled walls and all the portraits of past illustrious Harvard men looking placidly down give one a sense of the continuity of life and the relative unimportance of the disasters that may befall the individual. I felt strangely cheered up, as though today's troubles would not last—surely there was hope.

Dad drove me back up to my apartment and then headed on home.

"Your mother will be anxious to have a report on you," he said.

We had hardly discussed the kidnapping at all, except for my story of Ronald Gore and Eve. We had talked of other things. He had, that is—Australia, Hong Kong, the Philippines . . .

I drew lines on my wall on into the night. And the eleven o'clock news, at last, had word from Ottawa of Roy Lissing. In trying to escape the police, he had plunged five floors from the roof of an apartment building. He had died of the fall.

I paced for hours, wondering whether any scrap of information had been discovered that would lead to Julie. Hoping someone would call and tell me there was good news.

After some coffee at two A.M. I went back to my drawing. I was on the third wall now, on which I'd begun the Biblioteca Nazionale, from my pictures of Florence.

When my morning *Times* came I learned that Lissing had been staying at the Wapawnet address with an expatriot American couple—a draft evader and his wife. The old connection with Warren Thayer was brought in, but there was no mention of a tie-up with what had happened yesterday to Hugo Praeger. If any link had been discovered between Roy and events here in New York, the paper didn't have it.

No ransom demand had as yet been received by the Thayer family.

Hugo Praeger was holding his own nicely. He would not be paralyzed, his doctors stated.

191

Just before the eight o'clock news that morning my phone rang.

It was George Cavanaugh.

"Thanks for the information on where to find Lissing. You heard?"

"That he's dead—yes."

"I know you're particularly anxious about Julie Thayer. Well, I'm sorry we've nothing new there. We were hoping we'd pick up some kind of a lead when they got Lissing. But the police have searched the apartment in Ottawa and found nothing more than some of those leaflets you told us he'd printed. Nothing on the body, either—no addresses or phone numbers."

"How about the couple he was staying with?"

"They appear to have been sympathetic with Lissing, and with Warren Thayer before that. But apparently they're not actively engaged in any movement. Don't seem to know anything about a plot to kill Praeger; don't know any of the people on this end of the conspiracy—whoever they are besides Gore. In other words, nothing that's of any help."

So finding Roy Lissing had been only a dead end.

15

I can picture it now to myself, of course—the place where she was held: the handsome building with its rather impressive stone entrance; the row of third-floor windows, with their elegant pediments, looking out over the river; the living room with its walls of books and comfortable bachelor furnishings. The room where they found her—I never saw it, but news photos of it were in all the papers—the large, high-ceilinged bathroom with its tub on claw feet, and its john with a pull chain. The window was high up, out of her reach, and it gave only on the blank wall of an air shaft. It was also barred. It was there that she had stayed, with her hands tied behind her, her mouth taped shut except when she ate.

Would I have been any better off knowing in what kind of place she was? Or that she slept on a mattress in a corner behind the door?

That was Thursday, that day. And she'd been taken on Monday. It seemed like years.

I would have called Frances, after I'd talked to Cavanaugh, to see how she was—but I thought it was too early for her. I'd go over later in the day.

It was more than twenty-four hours since I'd had any sleep. Food might help, I thought, so I slugged down some orange juice and toasted a couple of frozen waffles which I ate with butter and jelly. Then I pulled the drapes closed on the city of Florence and collapsed on top of my bed.

The phone waked me.

I found it with difficulty—after first trying to turn off my alarm clock.

"Hello?" I said fuzzily.

"Lex?" I didn't recognize the voice.

"Yes." My head was clearing. "This is Lex." The digital clock by the phone said 10:47. Had to be A.M., still—light seeped in around the edges of the drapes.

"This is Gary."

There had been only one Gary in my life. We'd shared an operating table. And a knitting needle and—

"Yes, Gary—" I was almost afraid to breathe for fear I'd frighten him off.

"Is your phone bugged?"

"I'm sure it's not." The possibility had never occurred to me.

"It might be. They might think a ransom call could come in to you."

"The police would have told me if it was bugged. It's her aunt's where they're waiting for the call. Probably at her father's house, too."

"We can't be sure . . ." he said uncertainly.

"Then do you want me to call you back? From another phone?"

"There's not time." He sounded very nervous.

"Gary—I can cope, whatever the problem. If there's a way to get Julie back safely—"

"Yes, that's what I want. Why I called. You're the only one I can trust, Lex. You were Warren's friend, and I know I can trust you. Not to louse me up? To keep the police out of it?"

"You can trust me, Gary. I'll do anything. Anything you say."

"Get thirty thousand dollars together. Unmarked bills, from different banks maybe, so you won't attract attention doing it?"

"Okay. No problem."

"It's not ransom. It's for me to get away. You see Ronald will kill me if he can find me—I've got to get clear away and hide."

"Yes. I understand that."

"This is our one chance—Julie's and mine. And we've only got today."

Horrible fear gripped me. Why did we only have today?

"Today. All right."

"Okay. Get the money. Make sure you're not followed—can you be positive?"

"I managed that before—in Montreal. I'll make *very* sure."

"Wait for me, beginning at two o'clock."

"Where?" I hoped he'd stopped worrying about the phone being bugged.

He hadn't. "Julie says—don't tell me the answer, just say whether you remember—where Warren—"

The operator cut in. "Ten cents, please, for the next—"

"Oh, Christ!" I heard him say. And wondered frantically whether he had more change.

"Gary—" I waited in a state of suspended animation. An eternity, and then I heard the wonderful musical chime that denoted money being dropped in the phone slot.

"Hello? Gary—where?"

"Where Warren chipped his tooth. You remember?"

"Right. I shoved him—that's why he fell and chipped it." The steps at the front entrance of the Museum of Natural History.

"Wait till I come. I don't know when that'll be."

"I'll wait."

"You see, I want out. I won't go along with having her killed."

195

His last words seemed to echo in my head after he'd hung up. Killed . . . having her killed . . . killed . . . killed . . .

At twenty of two I was standing south of the steps to the Museum of Natural History, on Central Park West. In the rain.

By now it seemed as if I'd spent half my life avoiding possible surveillance. My Canadian training had stood me in good stead, and I'd found myself slipping back into my old paranoia as though it had never left me.

I started out in my car. Let them look for me in it—that wasn't where I would be. I wove in and out of traffic, first on the East River Drive and then through the busy wet streets, and parked near a convenient phone booth.

From there I called my father. Luckily he was in his office, downtown, and I told him I needed thirty thousand dollars in bills that couldn't be traced.

"Isn't this a job for the police, Lex?" he asked. He hadn't needed to inquire what the money was for.

"No, Dad. I gave my word. I know this fellow. He's trusting me. Promise you won't try to be clever and safeguard me somehow—have me followed or anything? It's Julie's life."

"I don't like it, but I promise."

"Thanks."

When I picked up the briefcase full of bills at his office an hour and a half later—after a deviously executed trip by subway—he looked at me with misty eyes.

"Be careful, Lex. You're all we have." I saw the caring in his face.

We've always been very close—my father and I.

"I'll be careful, Dad. You'll keep your word, now, not to tell the police, or the F.B.I.—"

"Have I ever gone back on my word?"

I shook my head. "That's why I can't, either. This is between Gary and me, and it'll have to stay that way."

Dad looked at me somberly and nodded. "Good luck."

196

Another carefully planned trip on the subway—stepping into a car at the last minute, and then getting off again and watching to see whether anyone else did the same. And the converse—getting off as soon as the train stopped, and belatedly getting back in—

Next I went to a Hertz office and rented a car. I thought it might come in handy.

I drove uptown then to Seventy-ninth Street and cruised around till I found a parking place two blocks from the museum.

And so I waited. Hardly fitting into the scene, with school children passing in or out, in groups, with their teachers.

Two o'clock came; two-ten and two-fifteen. No Gary.

We've only got today—

Had my phone been bugged? I'd had no time to check—and doubted anyway whether I'd know a bug if I saw one. It didn't matter now; we had our meeting place.

Warren's tooth. It hadn't been just chipped—broken was more like it; he'd had to have it capped. (Probably one of the things that had been helpful in identifying him, up in the Laurentians.)

We'd been horsing around that day. We were what—ten? Eleven? I'd shoved him and he had fallen. Hit his tooth on the step—the left front upper. Julie had been with us that time—

Julie . . .

Two-twenty-five.

Old Badger. We had come here often during our Indian period, to study the exhibits of Indian life, and gaze into the glass cases containing the rows and rows of arrowheads. And had admired the great whale—that unfortunately had been dismantled now.

Odd how, when your friend has died, he is complete. Whatever he was going to be is finished. He will not change. And it was as I stood there by the steps we'd so often gone up and down that it came to me for the first time—Warren belonged

197

now, as he never had in life, to the people who had known him. Perhaps that was as close as anyone came to life after death: to be remembered.

It was nearly three o'clock when I saw Gary. He was standing on the corner, at Seventy-ninth Street, looking carefully around for lurking police. He was fatter than when I'd seen him last (compulsive eater? consuming in anxiety?)—his windbreaker hung open, showing the flesh bulged in the shirt and pants that had grown too small.

I headed for him at once. He saw me coming, and made a sickly smile.

"Hello, Gary."

He looked absolutely terrified.

"I've got a car parked nearby," I said. "If that will help matters any. Not mine—I didn't want the police spotting the license. It's rented."

"Okay. Yeh, that'll—that'll be fine." He licked his rather thick lips nervously.

"This way. And I wasn't followed. I've been in and out of subway cars all over Manhattan. So relax."

"Okay. Too late now, if anything slips up. I'm here."

"We'll be all right." I piloted him to my parked car.

"Up the West Side Highway," he directed. "It's near Columbia University." He bulged into the passenger seat.

I headed west.

"Is Julie all right?" I was finally able to ask it. "I mean, so far."

"Yes. She's fine. I like her, you know. Don't want anything to happen to her. All this is more than I bargained for—kidnapping? This was to be purely a political matter. Kill Praeger, that was all. And Ronald was going to do that—the rest of us were just to be lookouts. Then Ronald sees Julie with Praeger—every day. 'Warren must have talked,' he said. 'The pigs know what we're planning, and they've got Julie Thayer lined up to try to spot me.'

"Well, the rest of us wanted to quit right then. Forget the idea of knocking off Praeger. Or wait till later. Not Ronald. It just made him mad. 'The little bitch!' he kept saying."

Once Gary started talking, it was as if the dam had broken. All the way uptown.

"Ronald had it all set up—this loft up the street from the newspaper building. He'd picked the lock. And a place for us to stay. He's got this sublet—apartment belongs to a friend of his who's abroad. He and Lucia and I are there—not Eve, she's staying with some friends in Brooklyn. And now we've got Julie, of course—

"We've been talking to Julie—me and Lucia have . . . Nothing's like it was, Lex—seems you can't even tell who your friends are. What Julie told us Roy did to Warren—the capsules. Warren was my friend, more than Roy. And for *him*—

"And Ronald. Ronald's not my friend. He's not *anybody's* friend that I can see. He's a bloody madman. I don't want to be responsible for anyone's murder. Not Julie Warren's, not Hugo Praeger's. If Warren was that much against killing Praeger, *I'm* against it!

"I think the movement's had it. It's like Warren said, at the last—we should take it slow. The time's not right for revolution —not in this country. In South America, maybe; in Asia; not here. Not yet."

Rain danced on the pavement, and the traffic crawled, snarled as it always is when it rains in New York. To our left were the brown polluted waters of the Hudson, to our right the dripping trees and shrubbery of the miles-long strip of park above the river. We got off the West Side Highway, onto Riverside Drive.

"So what do we do when we get to the apartment?" I asked. "Will Gore be there?"

"I hope not. I'll have to go in and see—then signal you. Ronald's gone off somewhere to buy another rifle. Lost his . . ."

"I know." He'd left his in the loft after shooting Praeger.

Gary half smiled into his three chins. "They almost had him, right after he shot Praeger. He got out fast—back entrance through an alley. But already the fuzz were stopping people. He was ready for them, though. Had false identification with him. They wrote down who they thought he was and let him go. That was the reason we had to snatch Julie, really; in case Ronald was picked up before he got clear, after the shooting. Julie could have identified him, and his fake driver's license and all wouldn't have done a thing for him.

"Oh—" he said, looking around, "it's the block after the next. We'd better find a place to park."

A station wagon was pulling out from the curb ahead of me, and I slid into the spot it vacated. "Is he carrying a gun now? Aside from the one he may buy?"

"He has one—automatic. He's been leaving it at the apartment."

"Where? I may need to know."

"Top drawer of the desk in the living room. It's by the windows."

As we sat there in the car and I asked him questions, Gary was getting more and more nervous. His little button eyes darted everywhere, afraid of what they might light on. (Ronald coming along the sidewalk?)

"Where does Lucia stand on getting Julie out?"

He licked his lips. "Well, that's just the trouble. She doesn't wish Julie any ill, but she won't go against Ronald. She's very loyal to the movement. I know she wants the whole thing to be over, really, so she can get back to Mick in Canada—Mick wasn't with Roy, or they'd have got him." Gary blinked his eyes and looked around him, and I began to wonder whether he wasn't putting off any action by continuing to talk.

"What do we do with Lucia then?" I asked him.

"Well. We'll go ahead. I'll go up there, and if Ronald's not back yet, I'll stand in front of the window and signal."

"How about Lucia?"

"She won't know what I'm doing—I'll just be looking out of the window. I'll have left the lobby door open—I can wedge something so it won't close—so you won't have to ring the bell. Just come up. Third floor front. Knock on the door. Two quick raps, one, then two again." He demonstrated on the dashboard. "Lucia will think it's Ronald, and she'll open the door. While she's doing that, I'll get the automatic out of the drawer."

"Where's Julie? What room?"

"Bathroom. First door to the right, down the little hall as you come in. She can't reach the window there to attract anyone's attention."

"Okay. So I take on Lucia? And you'll back me up with the automatic?"

"Sure."

"What if Ronald's there?"

"Wait. Keep enough out of sight that he won't notice you if *he* comes to the window."

"Better give me a distinctive signal so I'll know it's *not* Ronald looking out at me."

"I'll cross my arms in front of me. Like an X."

That was as much planning as there seemed to be time for.

"Better get going then," I said.

"When do I get the money?" He eyed the briefcase. Not for the first time.

"When I see Julie. I'll bring the money up with me."

We got out of the car and walked up a block, the fat boy swiveling his head about in search of Ronald. As we crossed the street, he pointed out the building.

"That one." A handsome stone front, with a lot of ornamental grillwork.

Gary picked out a tree, across Riverside, behind which I could stand. "The end window, there. Left end. Third floor." Lights were on in the apartment because of the dark day.

And if something went wrong, I wondered—"Why did you

201

say it has to be today?"

The question seemed to steady him a little. He squared his shoulders. Though his chins quivered, detracting from the manful effect. "Because tonight Ronald's going to take her down to the river and drown her."

I swallowed hard before I could speak. "What if Ronald's there now, and doesn't leave?"

"Then our deal's off, come about dark." He studied me, with the water dripping down on him from the leaves above us. A look of cunning came into the button eyes. "Don't think you can go for the police. If I look out and you're gone from here, and I haven't signaled you to come up, I'll drown her early. Myself. In the bathtub. That'll be easy—her mouth's taped shut now, you see, and her hands tied behind her back . . ."

My mouth was so dry I could hardly speak. "I won't go for the police. But look. If it goes to sunset, as you say, I'll jump him when you all come out with her. Before you get to the river."

He shook his head. Slowly. "Wouldn't do any good. He plans to drown her first in the bathtub anyway. To make sure. *Then* take her down."

Tight-lipped, I stared at him.

"I'll wait," I said.

He nodded.

I watched him trudge to the entrance—stooping once to pick up something that lay in the grass. A stick to wedge in the door.

Briefcase in hand, I took my position behind the tree.

Gary was only bluffing, I was sure. About drowning her himself. But if Ronald was there—and I certainly believed he planned to get rid of her, as too dangerous to keep any longer —he might go ahead anytime now with the initial step in the bathtub.

He might have done it already.

*   *   *

202

Things did not go according to plan.

I watched Gary go up the steps and open the heavy glass door, with its ornamental grillwork. Inside, I knew, he would unlock the second door with his key, and leave it propped open for me.

I waited—visualizing him climbing two sets of stairs. Or was there an elevator? I prayed that Ronald wasn't back yet.

Three or four minutes must have passed, and gusts of rain swept the street, the sidewalks, the fronts of the buildings. My eyes were glued to the window, third floor, left end.

Where was he? I imagined Lucia creating some difficulty; or Ronald taking Gary by the scruff of the neck and demanding to know where he had been—

Okay. There he was, at the window. With his arms crossed.

I slipped from behind my tree. But as I started across the street, I was hit a glancing blow from the side by a kid on a bicycle, who came whizzing soundlessly out of nowhere. He sprawled on the pavement, tangled in his bike, and I landed on one knee.

The boy gave me a dirty look, said something obscene I didn't catch all of, and in a minute had mounted and gone on.

As I reached to retrieve the briefcase that had flown out of my hand, I happened to glance up. Directly in front of me, about to go up the steps of the building where Julie was held, I saw Ronald Gore. I caught only a glimpse, between two parked cars, of the ugly naked head, the curly lips. He hadn't seen me, as he came around the corner from the side street, because I'd been kneeling on the pavement.

If I could catch him before he got inside . . . But already it was too late for that. As I crossed the sidewalk, the grilled door swung shut behind him. And the other door was propped open. Damn!

It never occurred to me to abort the mission. Now was

203

probably my only chance to get into the apartment before it was too late.

I went on into the entrance to the building. And damn him, he'd taken the stick out of the inner door and it was locked.

I rang about six apartments—none of them on three. Someone pressed the buzzer for the door, and I went through. I bounded up the stairs.

The tenant in two rear had an eye to the crack of the door, which was held partly shut by two chains.

"Call the police—" I hissed to the eye. And hurried on.

Elevator doors were just closing on the third floor as I started up the next flight. I went quietly, not to alert him, and I could hear his footsteps—just barely—above me. The hall floors were asphalt-tiled—no carpet.

He was standing at the door, at the front, when I arrived on the third floor. He turned and saw me, and at that moment Lucia opened the apartment door.

I rushed him, and we were both carried over the threshold.

I remember Lucia's astonished face. And Gary's—sick-looking as he stood in the book-walled living room, the automatic sagging in his hand.

Gary was useless—that was obvious. But the gun was an essential.

Ronald didn't yet realize that he'd had a mutiny in his ranks —and then I knew that he'd never find it out: Gary would be on his side. This was three against one, and I had to get the automatic from Gary before one of the others did.

I hit Ronald solidly on the jaw this time—with a jar that went tingling to my shoulder. He staggered, but came back with a blow that almost sent me out the open door. I caught the frame with the hand that had just dropped the briefcase, and catapulted myself into the room again.

The struggle became a wrestling match. I don't know which of us would have won—I was bigger and stronger, but he was more skilled. But we fell, the two of us, and Ronald struck his head on a large cast-metal lion that stood on the floor next to the fireplace. He was momentarily stunned.

As I got to my feet, I looked around at Gary. He had backed away from the conflict and was trying to edge toward the outer door—his problem being that I was partially in his way. He still had the automatic, but I think he'd forgotten he held it.

I stepped over to him and gestured that he should give the weapon to me. He hesitated, drawing back and away, the gun coming up to point vaguely in my direction. His gaze shifted over to Ronald, who was painfully pulling himself to a sitting position, propped on one hand.

"Give me the gun," I panted. But he just looked at me, pointing it more surely now.

"Give it to me," I said again. "And take your money and get out. I've called the police."

He hadn't the guts to fire, I thought. I reached for the barrel, not knowing whether he mightn't squeeze the trigger out of sheer nervousness.

My hand closed on the metal, and I deflected the gun's aim downward. Limply, Garry's fat, sweaty fingers surrendered their hold.

He had barely let go when a chopping blow to my wrist caused me to drop what I'd been at such pains to acquire.

Lucia—who had come around behind me.

I hadn't had time even to think of her since she'd stepped backward as I came in; till I saw her now, picking up the automatic from where it lay.

She was quick. She snatched it and sprang back. But before she could take aim, I made a grab for her arm.

The noise of the report was deafening. Nerve-shattering.

Before the sound had stopped reverberating within the narrow confines of the room, I was falling. My head twisted to one side, a split second before I struck the carpeted floor, and I saw that it was Gary who'd been hit by the shot; not I. He'd been hit in the stomach.

I had fallen because as I moved toward Lucia, Ronald had tripped me.

The scene ended for me there. Either Lucia or Ronald hit me over the head with something and knocked me out.

One of my last thoughts was to wonder whether the eye downstairs had called the police.

16

I barely missed the police, it seems, when I slid off into unconsciousness. They had had the apartment staked out since a little after Gary had left to meet me at the Museum of Natural History. Some information had after all been dug up in Ottawa: the telephone company record of a call to Manhattan, made from the apartment where Roy Lissing had stayed. A check in New York revealed that the person to whom the phone number belonged had sublet his apartment, at the beginning of September, to a friend whose name was not known to the landlord. A pair of plainclothesmen had taken up a vigil nearby.

They had seen Ronald go in; had recognized him. But they had waited. They preferred not to try to get Julie out while he was there.

When the shot had been fired, however, they moved in.

I came to in the hospital.

My father was sitting by the bed.

"Is she all right?" I asked when I was able to form the words.

"I hear she's fine. She's still with the police. Now you're supposed to keep quiet. You've got a concussion."

"Tell me—what you can . . ." I had a whopping pain in my

207

skull, and a deep feeling of depression to go with it. So Julie was safe now, but I was right back where I had been before: without her.

My father told me what he could. It wasn't much. Gore had been taken into custody, and Lucia, too. Gary had died en route to the hospital; thirty thousand dollars couldn't do anything for him now.

I went to sleep. When I woke again, my mother was there, in place of Dad, in the armchair. She smiled and wouldn't talk to me because she said I was supposed to keep quiet. And the next time I opened my eyes, I was looking at Julie.

"You're back," I croaked, and she nodded. She was standing by the bed. She leaned down and kissed me, and her soft dark hair swung against my cheek.

"Not just out of gratitude, I hope—"

"Oh, no." Her fingers smoothed my forehead. "All this time I've been shut up there, with my mouth taped, the only thing that mattered—if they ever let me go—was getting back to you."

I pulled her down to me. My hands moved over her warm, living back, and our lips met and obliterated the bitterness, the loneliness, the agony, of the days gone by.

Praeger recovered. Getting shot won him a lot of sympathizers, and his chances in the election this year look good.

Ronald Gore will be tried for kidnapping and for the attempted murder of Hugo Praeger. Although the rifle with which he'd shot Praeger was not in his possession, since he'd abandoned it in the loft, Gore's fingerprints were found on it. And Lucia turned state's evidence—the only chance she would have of seeing the light of day outside of prison walls before middle age. Lucia Kolesik, her name was.

Eve was not picked up. Nor Mick. Maybe they're forming a new nucleus of the movement—somewhere. Though I doubt it. There are other subversive groups around, as we all know; but

208

that one would seem to have had its back broken.

And now to Oliver Thayer—

Julie had not seen a paper during her captivity. I showed her the clippings about the death of Philip Theobald. Not because I was still trying to prove my case against her father, but because I was troubled by the issues it presented. Julie had loved Warren—

"You're sure this is the man—that you saw him in my father's office that day, and again in Montreal—" We were back in my apartment, the Sunday after all the excitement.

"I'm sure."

She told me, then, the rest of the Theobald story.

"If my father wanted to find a man whom he could control completely—who could never get back at him—Phil Theobald was the man.

"Years ago when Mr. Theobald was doing fund raising for Downing University, there was a discrepancy of some kind in his accounts. Daddy, being involved with the Downing finances because of the medical school, was the one who discovered that Theobald had embezzled—I guess thousands. The whole thing was kept quiet, but the man was dismissed from his post, and got out of fund raising after that.

"Then when Richie was at prep school he ran across Mark Theobald. Daddy warned him to keep clear of Mark—that Mark's father was a crook. But Richie and the boy stayed friends.

"I'll tell you now—I didn't want to before—about the trouble they were in. It was a drug thing, in the first place. Mark was the supplier, Richie was using. Heroin. What happened involved a third boy—younger. Mark had to talk him into it—into sniffing heroin. This was in Richie's room, and Richie was recording the whole thing on his tape machine. For kicks, I guess. Well, the younger boy got an overdose and died.

"As I told you, Daddy and Mr. Theobald went up together to get things glossed over. The school didn't want the scandal,

209

nor did the parents of the dead boy, and they succeeded in hushing it all up. But Richie thinks Daddy has his recording of the whole affair; he was afraid to ask him, but didn't know what else could have become of it. If he's right, my father had a complete and devastating hold on Phil Theobald—you know, 'Do what I say or your son will be indicted for murder.' "

"What shall we do then, Julie—about your father?" I finally asked. "Anything?"

"Nothing we do will benefit Warren. But to look the other way and pretend we don't know how his death may have come about is—is a thing I couldn't live with. Even though it wasn't the bullet that killed him, but a blow on the head. It was the shooting that set the whole thing in motion . . .

"While I was being held I thought a lot. About your accusing my father; about why I got so mad at you. When I broke our engagement I was partly putting off thinking about what you had said. Because it *never* sounded impossible to me, really. But your indictment was of me as well—daughter of a murderer?"

"I'm sorry. That's not what I meant, and you know it."

"But your parentage is part of your identity . . . I couldn't help believing that. And then I suppose it was family loyalty, my getting so angry—I felt I'd be a traitor not to."

She made a self-deprecating gesture. "I was clinging to the past. So many years I wanted to be with my father and couldn't —or wouldn't—because of Christine. My father fixation is probably larger than life . . . I came to terms with all that, you see, during my captivity."

And so it was all right with Julie for me to go to the F.B.I. with what I knew.

But first we told her father. She would have it no other way.

We walked cold into his office. I have never been so terrified.

Beaming, Oliver crossed the big room toward us. But Julie stopped him in his tracks.

"Daddy—is it true that you sent Phil Theobald to Canada,

after Lex, to kill Warren?"

The light died in his eyes and his face turned slowly to the color of putty. He was indeed stopped in his tracks and he didn't move a muscle. Not a twitch of an eyelid or the tremor of a finger.

He breathed in and lifted his shoulders slightly. "Won't you sit down—" He led us over to the comfortable seating arrangement of long sofa and deep chairs by the gray glass wall that faced across Park Avenue.

We all sat down, and he glanced from one to the other of us. "You were saying?" We might have been members of some committee on which he served, or fund solicitors asking for a donation to charity.

"We felt we should tell you," I said, "that I'm going to the F.B.I. with the information that Theobald was tailing me in Montreal; and that I'd seen him here, in your outer office, the day you asked me to go and search for Warren."

"Go ahead. If you can close the case for them—" He shrugged. "Phil Theobald is dead, in any event."

"But *you* sent him to Montreal," Julie said stubbornly.

"Did I? Why would I do that?"

"Because you hated Uncle Stuart, and you've hated Warren even more—not only because he was Stuart's son but because you felt he was a disgrace to the sacrosanct name of Thayer—"

"Perhaps I should go and wipe out poor Frances, too," he suggested. "Make a clean sweep of the family, now that they've won our old private battle—alienated my daughter completely at last, after all these years of only doing a half-assed job of it."

He got up from his chair. His deep-set eyes glittered with anger. "You've said your piece, both of you. You may go now."

Julie stumbled to her feet. There were tears in her eyes. "You don't even *deny* it?" And I knew then the real reason she had come—she'd hoped, in spite of everything, that he could make her believe in his innocence.

211

"I wouldn't dignify your silly maunderings with a denial!"

I took Julie's arm and we made our way toward the door.

"May your cousin Warren rest in an unquiet grave," he said in tones of vitriol. "And both of you, too—when the time comes."

I told George Cavanaugh all that I knew of the Theobald story.

We waited.

On a day in late November I sat in Cavanaugh's office.

"The last week of June," he said, "Philip Theobald drove up to Canada on a fishing trip. But we don't know where he stayed, where he went. He had a station wagon. Could have slept in it and not registered anywhere. He came home a couple of weeks after the shooting of young Thayer.

"However, we cannot place him in Montreal. At any time."

"What about the night clerk at the Hôtel Genève? He—"

Cavanaugh shook his head. "Man's dead."

"Dead?" I said, startled. "How did he die?"

"He wasn't murdered, if that's what you're thinking. Died in the hospital of a ruptured appendix. So that's that. And no one at the Queen Elizabeth remembers seeing Theobald. If he was there.

"One interesting thing—Theobald was always short of money, according to everyone who knew him. Expensive tastes, lived up everything he earned. But when he died, he had fifty thousand in cash in his safe-deposit box. No record of where it came from."

"From knocking off Warren."

"Possible. But there's no proof."

"The fifty thousand was probably in advance, with more promised on completion of the job. But there would have been no evidence that Warren was dead till the body was identified —so payment was held up. Oliver's a busy man; probably the

212

first chance he had to make a date with Theobald, after Warren was found, was that night—the night Philip Theobald was killed."

"That's two weeks elapsed there, you know, from the time Warren Thayer's body was found to the date on which Theobald was killed."

"It had to be a time when Oliver Thayer was alone. When would that be, when he comes and goes in a chauffeured limousine? With Irwin Kuhn keeping track of his every move?"

"And he was doing without his chauffeur at the time Theobald was killed—yes, I know that. But no one saw a red Porsche in that section of Scarsdale that night. The Scarsdale police have checked."

"Which doesn't mean it wasn't there."

"No," said Cavanaugh, "it doesn't. But you know my advice to you?"

"I can guess."

"Forget this whole thing. Theobald may have shot Warren Thayer, but we have no proof. Oliver Thayer could have commissioned the job, and then murdered Theobald afterward, personally; but we can't prove it, the Scarsdale police can't prove it, the New York City police can't prove it. The weapon's never been found, either, with which Warren was shot. Theobald had a closetful of guns—a hunter, you know. But if he had a thirty-two automatic, he must have gotten rid of it.

"No—take my advice. Forget the whole thing."

The father did not give the bride away. For the second time in her life, Julie eloped. But this time the marriage was not annulled.

As my Dad says, if all the crimes committed by the impeccable high and mighty—whether they are in business, professions, or politics—were exposed tomorrow, there'd be an awful lot of office space for rent.

213

You don't think Oliver did it? . . . The majority of murders are committed by a person known to the victim. And of these, statistics show that in the larger percentage of cases the killer is a relative of the deceased. Ever since Cain and Abel . . .

Blood is thicker than water.